Richard Harding Davis

The Exiles and Other Stories

Richard Harding Davis

The Exiles and Other Stories

ISBN/EAN: 9783743367432

Manufactured in Europe, USA, Canada, Australia, Japa

Cover: Foto ©Andreas Hilbeck / pixelio.de

Manufactured and distributed by brebook publishing software (www.brebook.com)

Richard Harding Davis

The Exiles and Other Stories

·THE EXILES ·
AND OTHER STORIES

BY

RICHARD HARDING DAVIS

ILLUSTRATED

NEW YORK AND LONDON
HARPER & BROTHERS
PUBLISHERS

TO

MY FRIEND

J. DAVIS BRODHEAD

CONTENTS

	PAGE
THE EXILES	1
THE WRITING ON THE WALL	67
THE RIGHT OF WAY	94
HIS BAD ANGEL	121
THE BOY ORATOR OF ZEPATA CITY	154
THE ROMANCE IN THE LIFE OF HEFTY BURKE	173
AN ANONYMOUS LETTER	201

ILLUSTRATIONS

RICHARD HARDING DAVIS . . . . *Frontispiece*

"STOPPING FOR HALF-HOURS AT A TIME BEFORE
A BAZAAR" . . . . *Facing page* 16

"'TO BE SHUT OFF FROM ALL OF THAT'" . " " 28

THE BOAR-HUNT . . . . " " 40

EXHIBIT "A"—CHARLECOTE HOUSE WITHOUT THE
BARRIER . . . . " " 100

"'YOU CAN'T GO THROUGH THERE, SIR!'" . . " " 106

THE ATTACK ON THE BARRIER . . . . . . " " 110

"MURRAY CLUNG TO THE SLEDGE-HAMMER" . . " " 114

WE ARRIVED AT THE BRIDGE. . . . . . . " " 118

"HOPELESSNESS AND REMORSE WERE THE MEAN-
ING OF THE MUSIC" . . . . " " 146

"THE GENTLEMEN OF THE JURY SAT QUITE MO-
TIONLESS" . . . . " " 170

"'THERE, NOW, DON'T YOU TAKE ON SO'" . . " " 172

"BURKE WATCHED HER WITH A DEEP INTEREST" " " 184

"'I AM NOT GOOD AT SAYING THINGS'" . . . " " 190

"'DO YOU KNOW THAT YOU HAVE AN ENEMY?'" " " 212

"VAN BIBBER PUT HIS HAT FIRMLY ON HIS
HEAD" . . . . " " 218

THE EXILES, AND OTHER STORIES

THE EXILES

I

THE greatest number of people in the world prefer the most highly civilized places of the world, because they know what sort of things are going to happen there, and because they also know by experience that those are the sort of things they like. A very few people prefer barbarous and utterly uncivilized portions of the globe for the reason that they receive while there new impressions, and because they like the unexpected better than a routine of existence, no matter how pleasant that routine may be. But the most interesting places of all to study are those in which the savage and the cultivated man lie down together and try to live together in unity. This is so because we can learn from such places just how far a man of cultivation lapses into barbarism when he associates with savages, and how far the remnants of his former civilization will have influence upon the barbarians among whom he has come to live.

There are many such colonies as these, and they are the most picturesque plague-spots on the

globe. You will find them in New Zealand and
at Yokohama, in Algiers, Tunis, and Tangier, and
scattered thickly all along the South American
coast-line wherever the law of extradition obtains
not, and where public opinion, which is one of
the things a colony can do longest without, is unknown. These are the unofficial Botany Bays and
Melillas of the world, where the criminal goes of
his own accord, and not because his government
has urged him to do so and paid his passage there.

This is the story of a young man who went to
such a place for the benefit he hoped it would be
to his health, and not because he had robbed any
one, or done a young girl an injury. He was the
only son of Judge Henry Howard Holcombe, of
New York. That was all that it was generally
considered necessary to say of him. It was not,
however, quite enough, for, while his father had
had nothing but the right and the good of his
State and country to think about, the son was further occupied by trying to live up to his father's
name. Young Holcombe was impressed by this
fact from his earliest childhood. It rested upon
him while at Harvard and during his years at the
law school, and it went with him into society and
into the courts of law. When he rose to plead a
case he did not forget, nor did those present forget, that his father while alive had crowded those
same halls with silent, earnest listeners; and
when he addressed a mass-meeting at Cooper
Union, or spoke from the back of a cart in the

East Side, some one was sure to refer to the fact that this last speaker was the son of the man who was mobbed because he had dared to be an abolitionist, and who later had received the veneration of a great city for his bitter fight against Tweed and his followers.

Young Holcombe was an earnest member of every reform club and citizens' league, and his distinguished name gave weight as a director to charitable organizations and free kindergartens. He had inherited his hatred of Tammany Hall, and was unrelenting in his war upon it and its handiwork, and he spoke of it and of its immediate downfall with the bated breath of one who, though amazed at the wickedness of the thing he fights, is not discouraged nor afraid. And he would listen to no half-measures. Had not his grandfather quarrelled with Henry Clay, and so shaken the friendship of a lifetime, because of a great compromise which he could not countenance? And was his grandson to truckle and make deals with this hideous octopus that was sucking the life-blood from the city's veins? Had he not but yesterday distributed six hundred circulars, calling for honest government, to six hundred possible voters, all the way up Fourth Avenue?— and when some flippant one had said that he might have hired a messenger-boy to have done it for him and so saved his energies for something less mechanical, he had rebuked the speaker with a reproachful stare and turned away in silence.

Life was terribly earnest to young Holcombe, and he regarded it from the point of view of one who looks down upon it from the judge's bench, and listens with a frown to those who plead its cause.   He was not fooled by it; he was alive to its wickedness and its evasions.   He would tell you that he knew for a fact that the window man in his district was a cousin of the Tammany candidate, and that the contractor who had the cleaning of the street to do was a brother-in-law of one of the Hall's sachems, and that the policeman on his beat had not been in the country eight months. He spoke of these damning facts with the air of one who simply tells you that much, that you should see how terrible the whole thing really was, and what he could tell if he wished.

In his own profession he recognized the trials of law-breakers only as experiments, which went to establish and explain a general principle.   And prisoners were not men to him, but merely the exceptions that proved the excellence of a rule. Holcombe would defend the lowest creature or the most outrageous of murderers, not because the man was a human being fighting for his liberty or life, but because he wished to see if certain evidence would be admitted in the trial of such a case.   Of one of his clients the judge, who had a daughter of his own, said, when he sentenced him, "Were there many more such men as you in the world, the women of this land would pray to God to be left childless."   And when some one asked Holcombe, with ill-concealed disgust, how he came to defend the man, he replied: "I wished to show the unreliability of expert testimony from medical men. Yes; they tell me the man was a very bad lot."

It was measures, not men, to Holcombe, and law and order were his twin goddesses, and "no compromise" his watchword.

"You can elect your man if you'll give me two thousand dollars to refit our club-room with," one of his political acquaintances once said to him. "We've five hundred voters on the rolls now, and the members vote as one man. You'd be saving the city twenty times that much if you keep Croker's man out of the job. You know *that* as well as I do."

"The city can better afford to lose twenty thousand dollars," Holcombe answered, "than we can afford to give a two-cent stamp for corruption."

"All right," said the heeler; "all right, Mr. Holcombe. Go on. Fight 'em your own way. If they'd agree to fight you with pamphlets and circulars you'd stand a chance, sir; but as long as they give out money and you give out reading-matter to people that can't read, they'll win, and I naturally want to be on the winning side."

When the club to which Holcombe belonged finally succeeded in getting the Police Commissioners indicted for blackmailing gambling-houses, Holcombe was, as a matter of course and of public congratulation, on the side of the law; and as Assistant District-Attorney—a position given him on account of his father's name and in the hope that it would shut his mouth—distinguished himself nobly.

Of the four commissioners, three were convicted — the fourth, Patrick Meakim, with admirable foresight having fled to that country from which few criminals return, and which is vaguely set forth in the newspapers as "parts unknown."

The trial had been a severe one upon the zealous Mr. Holcombe, who found himself at the end of it in a very bad way, with nerves unstrung and brain so fagged that he assented without question when his doctor exiled him from New York by ordering a sea voyage, with change of environment and rest at the other end of it. Some one else suggested the northern coast of Africa and Tangier, and Holcombe wrote minute directions to the secretaries of all of his reform clubs urging continued efforts on the part of his fellow-workers, and sailed away one cold winter's morning for Gibraltar. The great sea laid its hold upon him, and the winds from the south thawed the cold in his bones, and the sun cheered his tired spirit. He stretched himself at full length reading those books which one puts off reading until illness gives one the right to do so, and so far as in him lay obeyed his doctor's first command, that he should forget New York and all that pertained to it. By the time he had reached the Rock he was up and ready to drift farther into the lazy irresponsible life of the Mediterranean coast, and he had forgotten his struggles against municipal misrule, and was at times for hours together utterly oblivious of his own personality.

A dumpy, fat little steamer rolled itself along like a sailor on shore from Gibraltar to Tangier, and Holcombe, leaning over the rail of its quarter-deck, smiled down at the chattering group of Arabs and Moors stretched on their rugs beneath him. A half-naked negro, pulling at the dates in the basket between his bare legs, held up a handful to him with a laugh, and Holcombe laughed back and emptied the cigarettes in his case on top of him, and laughed again as the ship's crew and the deck passengers scrambled over one another and shook out their voluminous robes in search of them. He felt at ease with the world and with himself, and turned his eyes to the white walls of Tangier with a pleasure so complete that it shut out even the thought that it was a pleasure.

The town seemed one continuous mass of white stucco, with each flat low-lying roof so close to the other that the narrow streets left no trace. To the left of it the yellow coast-line and the green olive-trees and palms stretched up against the sky, and beneath him scores of shrieking blacks fought in their boats for a place beside the steamer's companion-way. He jumped into

one of these open wherries and fell sprawling
among his baggage, and laughed lightly as a boy
as the boatman set him on his feet again, and then
threw them from under him with a quick stroke of
the oars.   The high, narrow pier was crowded with
excited customs officers in ragged uniforms and
dirty turbans, and with a few foreign residents
looking for arriving passengers.   Holcombe had
his feet on the upper steps of the ladder, and was
ascending slowly.   There was a fat, heavily built
man in blue serge leaning across the railing of the
pier.   He was looking down, and as his eyes met
Holcombe's face his own straightened into lines
of amazement and most evident terror.   Holcombe
stopped at the sight, and stared back wondering.
And then the lapping waters beneath him and the
white town at his side faded away, and he was
back in the hot, crowded court-room with this
man's face before him.   Meakim, the fourth of the
Police Commissioners, confronted him, and saw in
his presence nothing but a menace to himself.

Holcombe came up the last steps of the stairs,
and stopped at their top.   His instinct and life's
tradition made him despise the man, and to this
was added the selfish disgust that his holiday
should have been so soon robbed of its character
by this reminder of all that he had been told to
put behind him.

Meakim swept off his hat as though it were
hurting him, and showed the great drops of sweat
on his forehead.

"For God's sake!" the man panted, "you can't touch me here, Mr. Holcombe. I'm safe here; they told me I'd be. You can't take me. You can't touch me."

Holcombe stared at the man coldly, and with a touch of pity and contempt. "That is quite right, Mr. Meakim," he said. "The law cannot reach you here."

"Then what do you want with me?" the man demanded, forgetful in his terror of anything but his own safety.

Holcombe turned upon him sharply. "I am not here on your account, Mr. Meakim," he said. "You need not feel the least uneasiness, and," he added, dropping his voice as he noticed that others were drawing near, "if you keep out of my way, I shall certainly keep out of yours."

The Police Commissioner gave a short laugh partly of bravado and partly at his own sudden terror. "I didn't know," he said, breathing with relief. "I thought you'd come after me. You don't wonder you give me a turn, do you? I *was* scared." He fanned himself with his straw hat, and ran his tongue over his lips. "Going to be here some time, Mr. District Attorney?" he added, with grave politeness.

Holcombe could not help but smile at the absurdity of it. It was so like what he would have expected of Meakim and his class to give every office-holder his full title. "No, Mr. Police Commissioner," he answered, grimly, and nodding to his boatmen, pushed his way after them and his trunks along the pier.

Meakim was waiting for him as he left the custom-house. He touched his hat, and bent the whole upper part of his fat body in an awkward bow. "Excuse me, Mr. District Attorney," he began.

"Oh, drop that, will you?" snapped Holcombe. "Now, what is it you want, Meakim?"

"I was only going to say," answered the fugitive, with some offended dignity, "that as I've been here longer than you, I could perhaps give you pointers about the hotels. I've tried 'em all, and they're no good, but the Albion's the best."

"Thank you, I'm sure," said Holcombe. "But I have been told to go to the Isabella."

"Well, that's pretty good, too," Meakim answered, "if you don't mind the tables. They keep you awake most of the night, though, and—"

"The tables? I beg your pardon," said Holcombe, stiffly.

"Not the eatin' tables; the roulette tables," corrected Meakim. "Of course," he continued, grinning, "if you're fond of the game, Mr. Holcombe, it's handy having them in the same house, but I can steer you against a better one back of the French Consulate. Those at the Hôtel Isabella's crooked."

Holcombe stopped uncertainly. "I don't know just what to do," he said. "I think I shall wait until I can see our consul here."

"Oh, he'll send you to the Isabella," said Meakim, cheerfully. "He gets two hundred dollars a week for protecting the proprietor, so he naturally caps for the house."

Holcombe opened his mouth to express himself, but closed it again, and then asked, with some misgivings, of the hotel of which Meakim had first spoken.

"Oh, the Albion. Most all the swells go there. It's English, and they cook you a good beefsteak. And the boys generally drop in for table d'hôte. You see, that's the worst of this place, Mr. Holcombe; there's nowhere to go evenings—no clubrooms nor theatre nor nothing; only the smoking-room of the hotel or that gambling-house; and they spring a double naught on you if there's more than a dollar up."

Holcombe still stood irresolute, his porters eying him from under their burdens, and the runners from the different hotels plucking at his sleeve.

"There's some very good people at the Albion," urged the Police Commissioner, "and three or four of 'em's New-Yorkers. There's the Morrises and Ropes, the Consul-General, and Lloyd Carroll—"

"Lloyd Carroll!" exclaimed Holcombe.

"Yes," said Meakim, with a smile, "he's here." He looked at Holcombe curiously for a moment, and then exclaimed, with a laugh of intelligence, "Why, sure enough, you were Mr. Thatcher's lawyer in that case, weren't you? It was you got him his divorce?"

Holcombe nodded.

"Carroll was the man that made it possible, wasn't he?"

Holcombe chafed under this catechism. "He was one of a dozen, I believe," he said; but as he moved away he turned and asked: "And Mrs. Thatcher. What has become of her?"

The Police Commissioner did not answer at once, but glanced up at Holcombe from under his half-shut eyes with a look in which there was a mixture of curiosity and of amusement. "You don't mean to say, Mr. Holcombe," he began, slowly, with the patronage of the older man and with a touch of remonstrance in his tone, "that you're *still* with the husband in that case?"

Holcombe looked coldly over Mr. Meakim's head. "I have only a purely professional interest in any one of them," he said. "They struck me as a particularly nasty lot. Good-morning, sir."

"Well," Meakim called after him, "you needn't see nothing of them if you don't want to. You can get rooms to yourself."

Holcombe did get rooms to himself, with a balcony overlooking the bay, and arranged with the proprietor of the Albion to have his dinner served at a separate table. As others had done this before, no one regarded it as an affront upon his society, and several people in the hotel made ad-

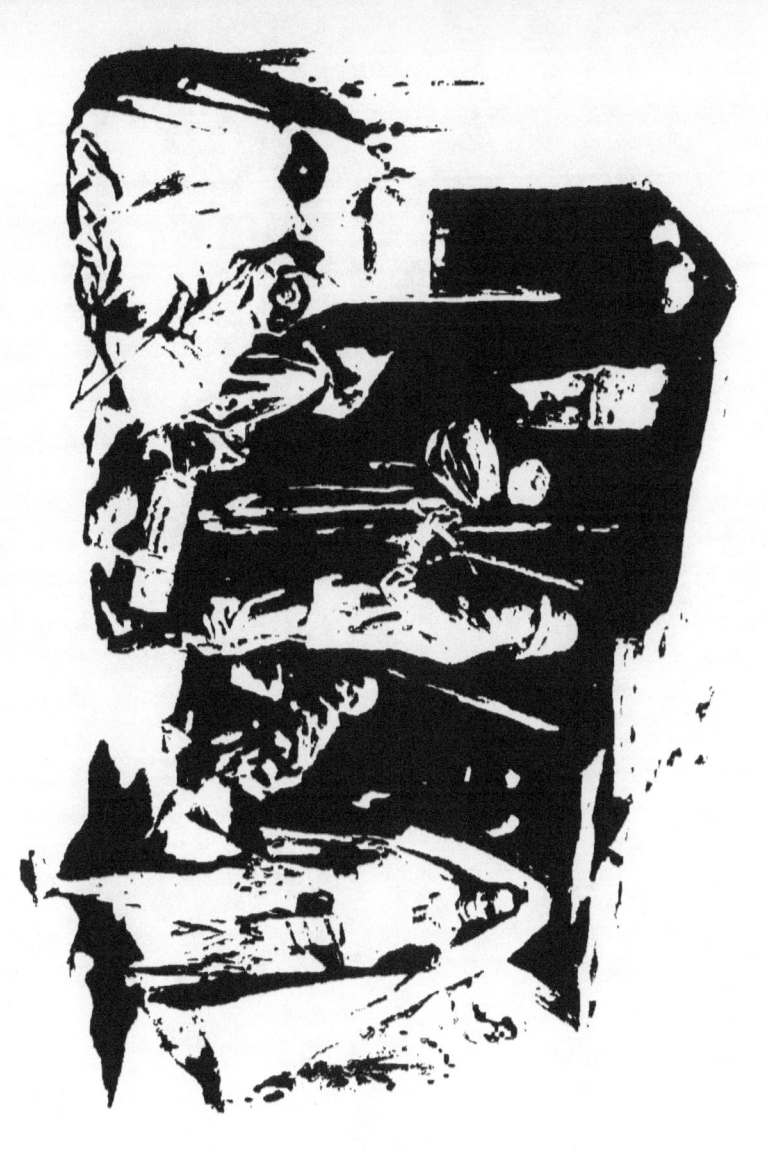

vances to him, which he received politely but
coldly. For the first week of his visit the town
interested him greatly, increasing its hold upon
him unconsciously to himself. He was restless
and curious to see it all, and rushed his guide
from one of the few show-places to the next with
an energy which left that fat Oriental panting.

But after three days Holcombe climbed the
streets more leisurely, stopping for half-hours at a
time before a bazaar, or sent away his guide altogether, and stretched himself luxuriously on the
broad wall of the fortifications. The sun beat
down upon him, and wrapped him into drowsiness.
From far afield came the unceasing murmur of the
market-place and the bazaars, and the occasional
cries of the priests from the minarets; the dark
blue sea danced and flashed beyond the white mar-
gin of the town and its protecting reef of rocks
where the sea-weed rose and fell, and above his
head the buzzards swept heavily, and called to one
another with harsh, frightened cries. At his side
lay the dusty road, hemmed in by walls of cactus,
and along its narrow length came lines of patient
little donkeys with jangling necklaces, led by wild-
looking men from the farm-lands and the desert,
and women muffled and shapeless, with only their
bare feet showing, who looked at him curiously
or meaningly from over the protecting cloth, and
passed on, leaving him startled and wondering.
He began to find that the books he had brought
wearied him. The sight of the type alone was

enough to make him close the covers and start
up restlessly to look for something less absorb-
ing. He found this on every hand, in the lazy
patience of the bazaars and of the markets, where
the chief service of all was that of only standing
and waiting, and in the farm-lands behind Tangier, where half-naked slaves drove great horned
buffalo, and turned back the soft, chocolate-col-
ored sod with a wooden plough. But it was a
solitary, selfish holiday, and Holcombe found himself wanting certain ones at home to bear him
company, and was surprised to find that of these
none were the men nor the women with whom his
interests in the city of New York were the most
closely connected. They were rather foolish people, men at whom he had laughed and whom he
had rather pitied for having made him do so, and
women he had looked at distantly as of a kind he
might understand when his work was over and
he wished to be amused. The young girls to
whom he was in the habit of pouring out his de-
nunciations of evil, and from whom he was accustomed to receive advice and moral support, he
could not place in this landscape. He felt uneasily that they would not allow him to enjoy it his
own way; they would consider the Moor histor-
ically as the invader of Catholic Europe, and
would be shocked at the lack of proper sanita-
tion, and would see the mud. As for himself, he
had risen above seeing the mud. He looked up
now at the broken line of the roof-tops against

the blue sky, and when a hooded figure drew
back from his glance he found himself murmur-
ing the words of an Eastern song he had read
in a book of Indian stories:

"Alone upon the house-tops, to the north
  I turn and watch the lightning in the sky,—
The glamour of thy footsteps in the north.
Come back to me, Beloved, or I die!

"Below my feet the still bazaar is laid.
  Far, far below, the weary camels lie—"

Holcombe laughed and shrugged his shoulders.
He had stopped half-way down the hill on which
stands the Bashaw's palace, and the whole of
Tangier lay below him like a great cemetery of
white marble. The moon was shining clearly
over the town and the sea, and a soft wind from
the sandy farm-lands came to him and played
about him like the fragrance of a garden. Something moved in him that he did not recognize,
but which was strangely pleasant, and which ran
to his brain like the taste of a strong liqueur. It
came to him that he was alone among strangers,
and that what he did now would be known but to
himself and to these strangers. What it was that
he wished to do he did not know, but he felt a
sudden lifting up and freedom from restraint.
The spirit of adventure awoke in him and tugged
at his sleeve, and he was conscious of a desire to
gratify it and to put it to the test.

"'Alone upon the house-tops,'" he began. Then he laughed and clambered hurriedly down the steep hill-side. "It's the moonlight," he explained to the blank walls and overhanging lattices, "and the place and the music of the song. It might be one of the Arabian nights, and I Haroun al Raschid. *And* if I don't get back to the hotel I shall make a fool of myself."

He reached the Albion very warm and breathless, with stumbling and groping in the dark, and instead of going immediately to bed told the waiter to bring him some cool drink out on the terrace of the smoking-room. There were two men sitting there in the moonlight, and as he came forward one of them nodded to him silently.

"Oh, good-evening, Mr. Meakim!" Holcombe said, gayly, with the spirit of the night still upon him. "I've been having adventures." He laughed, and stooped to brush the dirt from his knickerbockers and stockings. "I went up to the palace to see the town by moonlight, and tried to find my way back alone, and fell down three times."

Meakim shook his head gravely. "You'd better be careful at night, sir," he said. "The governor has just said that the Sultan won't be responsible for the lives of foreigners at night 'unless accompanied by soldier and lantern.'"

"Yes, and the legations sent word that they wouldn't have it," broke in the other man. "They said they'd hold him responsible anyway."

There was a silence, and Meakim moved in some slight uneasiness. "Mr. Holcombe, do you know Mr. Carroll?" he said.

Carroll half rose from his chair, but Holcombe was dragging another towards him, and so did not have a hand to give him.

"How are you, Carroll?" he said, pleasantly.

The night was warm, and Holcombe was tired after his rambles, and so he sank back in the low wicker chair contentedly enough, and when the first cool drink was finished he clapped his hands for another, and then another, while the two men sat at the table beside him and avoided such topics as would be unfair to any of them.

"And yet," said Holcombe, after the first half-hour had passed, "there must be a few agreeable people here. I am sure I saw some very nice-looking women to-day coming in from the fox-hunt. And very well gotten up, too, in Karki habits. And the men were handsome, decent - looking chaps—Englishmen, I think."

"Who does he mean? Were you at the meet to-day?" asked Carroll.

The Tammany chieftain said no, that he did not ride—not after foxes, in any event. "But I saw Mrs. Hornby and her sister coming back," he said. "They had on those linen habits."

"Well, now, there's a woman who illustrates just what I have been saying," continued Carroll. "You picked her out as a self - respecting, nice-looking girl—and so she is—but she wouldn't like to have to tell all she knows. No, they are all pretty much alike. They wear low-neck frocks, and the men put on evening dress for dinner, and they ride after foxes, and they drop in to five-o'clock tea, and they all play that they're a lot of gilded saints, and it's one of the rules of the game that you must believe in the next man, so that he will believe in you. I'm breaking the rules myself now, because I say 'they' when I ought to say 'we.' We're none of us here for our health, Holcombe, but it pleases us to pretend we are. It's a sort of give and take. We all sit around at dinner-parties and smile and chatter, and those English talk about the latest news from 'town,' and how they mean to run back for the season or the hunting. But they know they don't dare go back, and they know that everybody at the table knows it, and that the servants behind them know it. But it's more easy that way. There's only a few of us here, and we've got to hang together or we'd go crazy."

"That's so," said Meakim, approvingly. "It makes it more sociable."

"It's a funny place," continued Carroll. The wine had loosened his tongue, and it was something to him to be able to talk to one of his own people again, and to speak from their point of view, so that the man who had gone through St. Paul's and Harvard with him would see it as such a man should. "It's a funny place, because, in spite of the fact that it's a prison, you grow to like it for its freedom. You can do things here you can't do in New York, and pretty much everything goes there, or it used to, where I hung out. But here you're just your own master, and there's no law and no religion and no relations nor newspapers to poke into what you do nor how you live. You can understand what I mean if you've ever tried living in the West. I used to feel the same way the year I was ranching in Texas. My family sent me out there to put me out of temptation; but I concluded I'd rather drink myself to death on good whiskey at Del's than on the stuff we got on the range, so I pulled my freight and came East again. But while I was there I was a little king. I was just as good as the next man, and he was no better than me. And though the life was rough, and it was cold and lonely, there was something in being your own boss that made you stick it out there longer than anything else did. It was like this, Holcombe." Carroll half rose from his chair and marked what he said with his finger. "Every time I took a step and my gun bumped against my hip, I'd straighten up and feel good and look for trouble. There was nobody to appeal to; it was just between me and him, and no one else had any say about it. Well, that's what it's like here. You see men come to Tangier on the run, flying from detectives or husbands or bank directors, men who have lived perfectly decent, commonplace lives up to the time they made their one bad break—which," Carroll added, in polite parenthesis, with a deprecatory wave of his hand towards Meakim and himself, "we are *all* likely to do some time, aren't we?"

"Just so," said Meakim.

"Of course," assented the District Attorney.

"But as soon as he reaches this place, Holcombe," continued Carroll, "he begins to show just how bad he is. It all comes out — all his viciousness and rottenness and blackguardism. There is nothing to shame it, and there is no one to blame him, and no one is in a position to throw the first stone." Carroll dropped his voice and pulled his chair forward with a glance over his shoulder. "One of those men you saw riding in from the meet to-day. Now, he's a German officer, and he's here for forging a note or cheating at cards or something quiet and gentlemanly, nothing that shows him to be a brute or a beast. But last week he had old Mulley Wazzam buy him a slave girl in Fez, and bring her out to his house in the suburbs. It seems that the girl was in love with a soldier in the Sultan's body-guard at Fez, and tried to run away to join him, and this man met her quite by accident as she was making her way south across the sand-hills. He was whip that day, and was hurrying out to the meet alone. He had some words with the girl first, and then took his whip —it was one of those with the long lash to it; you know what I mean—and cut her to pieces with it, riding her down on his pony when she tried to run, and heading her off and lashing her around

the legs and body until she fell; then he rode on
in his damn pink coat to join the ladies at Mango's
Drift, where the meet was, and some Riffs found
her bleeding to death behind the sand-hills. That
man held a commission in the Emperor's own body-
guard, and that's what Tangier did for *him*."

Holcombe glanced at Meakim to see if he
would verify this, but Meakim's lips were tightly
pressed around his cigar, and his eyes were half
closed.

"And what was done about it?" Holcombe
asked, hoarsely.

Carroll laughed, and shrugged his shoulders.
"Why, I tell you, and you whisper it to the next
man, and we pretend not to believe it, and call
the Riffs liars. As I say, we're none of us here
for our health, Holcombe, and a public opinion
that's manufactured by *déclassée* women and men
who have run off with somebody else's money
and somebody else's wife isn't strong enough to
try a man for beating his own slave."

"But the Moors themselves?" protested Holcombe. "And the Sultan? She's one of his
subjects, isn't she?"

"She's a woman, and women don't count for
much in the East, you know; and as for the Sultan, he's an ignorant black savage. When the
English wanted to blow up those rocks off the
western coast, the Sultan wouldn't let them. He
said Allah had placed them there for some good
reason of His own, and it was not for man to in-

terfere with the works of God. That's the sort of a Sultan he is." Carroll rose suddenly and walked into the smoking - room, leaving the two men looking at each other in silence.

"That's right," said Meakim, after a pause. "He give it to you just as it is, but I never knew him to kick about it before. We're a fair field for missionary work, Mr. Holcombe, all of us—at least, some of us are." He glanced up as Carroll came back from out of the lighted room with an alert, brisk step. His manner had changed in his absence.

"Some of the ladies have come over for a bit of supper," he said. " Mrs. Hornby and her sister and Captain Reese. The *chef's* got some birds for us, and I've put a couple of bottles on ice. It will be like Del's—hey ? A small hot bird and a large cold bottle. They sent me out to ask you to join us. They're in our rooms." Meakim rose leisurely and lit a fresh cigar, but Holcombe moved uneasily in his chair. "You'll come, won't you ?" Carroll asked. " I'd like you to meet my wife."

Holcombe rose irresolutely and looked at his watch. " I'm afraid it's too late for me," he said, without raising his face. " You see, I'm here for my health. I—"

" I beg your pardon," said Carroll, sharply.

"Nonsense, Carroll!" said Holcombe. " I didn't mean *that*. I meant it literally. I can't risk midnight suppers yet. My doctor's orders

are to go to bed at nine, and it's past twelve
now. Some other time, if you'll be so good; but
it's long after my bedtime, and—"

"Oh, certainly," said Carroll, quietly, as he
turned away. "Are you coming, Meakim?"

Meakim lifted his half-empty glass from the
table and tasted it slowly until Carroll had left
them, then he put the glass down, and glanced
aside to where Holcombe sat looking out over the
silent city. Holcombe raised his eyes and stared
at him steadily.

"Mr. Holcombe—" the fugitive began.

"Yes," replied the lawyer.

Meakim shook his head. "Nothing," he said.
"Good-night, sir."

Holcombe's rooms were on the floor above Carroll's, and the laughter of the latter's guests and
the tinkling of glasses and silver came to him as
he stepped out upon his balcony. But for this the
night was very still. The sea beat leisurely on
the rocks, and the waves ran up the sandy coast
with a sound as of some one sweeping. The music
of women's laughter came up to him suddenly,
and he wondered hotly if they were laughing at
him. He assured himself that it was a matter of
indifference to him if they were. And with this
he had a wish that they would not think of him
as holding himself aloof. One of the women began to sing to a guitar, and to the accompaniment
of this a man and a young girl came out upon the
balcony below, and spoke to each other in low,

3

earnest tones, which seemed to carry with them the feeling of a caress. Holcombe could not hear what they said, but he could see the curve of the woman's white shoulders and the light of her companion's cigar as he leaned upon the rail with his back to the moonlight and looked into her face. Holcombe felt a sudden touch of loneliness and of being very far from home. He shivered slightly as though from the cold, and stepping inside closed the window gently behind him.

Although Holcombe met Carroll several times during the following day, the latter obviously avoided him, and it was not until late in the afternoon that Holcombe was given a chance to speak to him again. Carroll was coming down the only street on a run, jumping from one rough stone to another, and with his face lighted up with excitement. He hailed Holcombe from a distance with a wave of the hand. "There's an American man-of-war in the bay," he cried; "one of the new ones. We saw her flag from the hotel. Come on!" Holcombe followed as a matter of course, as Carroll evidently expected that he would, and they reached the end of the landing-pier together, just as the ship of war ran up and broke the square red flag of Morocco from her main-mast and fired her salute.

"They'll be sending a boat in by-and-by," said Carroll, "and we'll have a talk with the men." His enthusiasm touched his companion also, and the sight of the floating atom of the great country

that was his moved him strongly, as though it were
a personal message from home. It came to him
like the familiar stamp, and a familiar handwrit-
ing on a letter in a far-away land, and made him
feel how dear his own country was to him and
how much he needed it. They were leaning side
by side upon the rail watching the ship's screws
turning the blue waters white, and the men running about the deck, and the blue-coated figures
on the bridge. Holcombe turned to point out
the vessel's name to Carroll, and found that his
companion's eyes were half closed and filled with
tears.

Carroll laughed consciously and coughed. "We
kept it up a bit too late last night," he said, "and
I'm feeling nervous this morning, and the sight of
the flag and those boys from home knocked me
out." He paused for a moment, frowning through
his tears and with his brow drawn up into many
wrinkles. "It's a terrible thing, Holcombe," he
began again, fiercely, "to be shut off from all of
that." He threw out his hand with a sudden gesture towards the man-of-war. Holcombe looked
down at the water and laid his hand lightly on his
companion's shoulder. Carroll drew away and
shook his head. "I don't want any sympathy,"
he said, kindly. "I'm not crying the baby act.
But you don't know, and I don't believe anybody
else knows, what I've gone through and what I've
suffered. You don't like me, Holcombe, and you
don't like my class, but I want to tell you some-

thing about my coming here. I want you to set them right about it at home. And I don't care whether it interests you or not," he said, with quick offence; "I want you to listen. It's about my wife."

Holcombe bowed his head gravely.

"You got Thatcher his divorce," Carroll continued. "And you know that he would never have got it but for me, and that everybody expected that I would marry Mrs. Thatcher when the thing was over. And I didn't, and everybody said I was a blackguard, and I was. It was bad enough before, but I made it worse by not doing the only thing that could make it any better. Why I didn't do it I don't know. I had some grand ideas of reform about that time, I think, and I thought I owed my people something, and that by not making Mrs. Thatcher my mother's daughter I would be saving her and my sisters. It was remorse, I guess, and I didn't see things straight. I know now what I should have done. Well, I left her and she went her own way, and a great many people felt sorry for her, and were good to her—not your people, nor my people; but enough were good to her to make her see as much of the world as she had used to. She never loved Thatcher, and she never loved any of the men you brought into that trial except one, and he treated her like a cur. That was myself. Well, what with trying to please my family, and loving Alice Thatcher all the time and not seeing her, and hating her too for bringing me into all that notoriety—for I blamed the woman, of course, as a man always will—I got to drinking, and then this scrape came and I had to run. I don't care anything about that row now, or what you believe about it. I'm here, shut off from my home, and that's a worse punishment than any damn lawyers can invent. And the man's well again. He saw I was drunk; but I wasn't so drunk that I didn't know he was trying to do me, and I pounded him just as they say I did, and I'm sorry now I didn't kill him."

Holcombe stirred uneasily, and the man at his side lowered his voice and went on more calmly:

"If I hadn't been a gentleman, Holcombe, or if it had been another cabman he'd fought with, there wouldn't have been any trouble about it. But he thought he could get big money out of me, and his friends told him to press it until he was paid to pull out, and I hadn't the money, and so I had to break bail and run. Well, you've seen the place. You've been here long enough to know what it's like, and what I've had to go through. Nobody wrote me, and nobody came to see me; not one of my own sisters even, though they've been in the Riviera all this spring—not a day's journey away. Sometimes a man turned up that I knew, but it was almost worse than not seeing any one. It only made me more homesick when he'd gone. And for weeks I used to walk up and down that beach there alone late in the night, until I got to thinking that the waves were talking to me, and I got queer in my head. I had to fight it just as I used to have to fight against whiskey, and to talk fast so that I wouldn't think. And I tried to kill myself hunting, and only got a broken collar-bone for my pains. Well, all this time Alice was living in Paris and New York. I heard that some English captain was going to marry her, and then I read in the Paris *Herald* that she was settled in the American colony there, and one day it gave a list of the people who'd been to a reception she gave. She could go where she pleased, and she had money in her own right, you know ; and she was being revenged on me every day. And I was here knowing it, and loving her worse than I ever loved anything on earth, and having lost the right to tell her so, and not able to go to her. Then one day some chap turned up from here and told her about me, and about how miserable I was, and how well I was being punished. He thought it would please her, I suppose. I don't know who he was, but I guess he was in love with her himself. And then the papers had it that I was down with the fever here, and she read about it. I *was* ill for a time, and I hoped it was going to carry me off decently, but I got up in a week or two, and one day I crawled down here where we're standing now to watch the boat come in. I was pretty weak from my illness, and I was bluer than I had ever been, and I didn't see anything but blackness and bit-

terness for me anywhere. I turned around when
the passengers reached the pier, and I saw a
woman coming up those stairs. Her figure and
her shoulders were so like Alice's that my heart
went right up into my throat, and I couldn't
breathe for it. I just stood still staring, and
when she reached the top of the steps she looked
up, breathing with the climb, and laughing ; and
she says, 'Lloyd, I've come to see you.' And I—
I was that lonely and weak that I grabbed her
hand, and leaned back against the railing, and cried
there before the whole of them. I don't think
she expected it exactly, because she didn't know
what to do, and just patted me on the shoulder,
and said, 'I thought I'd run down to cheer you
up a bit ; and I've brought Mrs. Scott with me
to chaperone us.' And I said, without stopping
to think : 'You wouldn't have needed any chap-
eron, Alice, if I hadn't been a cur and a fool.
If I had only asked what I can't ask of you now ;'
and, Holcombe, she flushed just like a little girl,
and laughed, and said, 'Oh, will you, Lloyd ?'
And you see that ugly iron chapel up there, with
the corrugated zinc roof and the wooden cross on
it, next to the mosque ? Well, that's where we
went first, right from this wharf before I let her
go to a hotel, and old Ridley, the English rector,
he married us, and we had a civil marriage too.
That's what she did for me. She had the whole
wide globe to live in, and she gave it up to
come to Tangier, because I had no other place

but Tangier, and she's made my life for me, and I'm happier here than I ever was before anywhere, and sometimes I think—I hope—that she is, too." Carroll's lips moved slightly, and his hands trembled on the rail. He coughed, and his voice was gentler when he spoke again. "And so," he added, "that's why I felt it last night when you refused to meet her. You were right, I know, from your way of thinking, but we've grown careless down here, and we look at things differently."

Holcombe did not speak, but put his arm across the other's shoulder, and this time Carroll did not shake it off. Holcombe pointed with his hand to a tall, handsome woman with heavy yellow hair who was coming towards them, with her hands in the pockets of her reefer. "There is Mrs. Carroll now," he said. "Won't you present me, and then we can row out and see the man-of-war?"

II

The officers returned their visit during the day, and the American Consul-General asked them all to a reception the following afternoon. The entire colony came to this, and Holcombe met many people, and drank tea with several ladies in riding-habits, and iced drinks with all of the men. He found it very amusing, and the situation appealed strongly to his somewhat latent sense of humor. That evening in writing to his sister he told of his rapid recovery in health, and of the possibility of his returning to civilization.

"There was a reception this afternoon at the Consul-General's," he wrote, "given to the officers of our man-of-war, and I found myself in some rather remarkable company. The consul himself has become rich by selling his protection for two hundred dollars to every wealthy Moor who wishes to escape the forced loans which the Sultan is in the habit of imposing on the faithful. For five hundred dollars he will furnish any one of them with a piece of stamped paper accrediting him as minister plenipotentiary from the United States to the Sultan's court. Of course the Sultan never receives them, and whatever object they may have had in taking the long journey to Fez is never accomplished. Some day some one of them will find out how he has been tricked, and will return to have the consul assassinated. This will be a serious loss to our diplomatic service. The consul's wife is a fat German woman who formerly kept a hotel here. Her brother has it now, and runs it as an annex to a gambling-house. Pat Meakim, the police commissioner that I indicted, but who jumped his bail, introduced me at the reception to the men, with apparently great self-satisfaction, as 'the pride of the New York Bar,' and Mrs. Carroll, for whose husband I obtained a divorce, showed her gratitude by presenting me to the ladies. It was a distinctly Gilbertian situation, and the people to whom they introduced me were quite as picturesquely disreputable as themselves. So you see—"

Holcombe stopped here and read over what he had written, and then tore up the letter. The one he sent in its place said he was getting better, but that the climate was not so mild as he had expected it would be.

Holcombe engaged the entire first floor of the hotel the next day, and entertained the officers and the residents at breakfast, and the Admiral made a speech and said how grateful it was to him and to his officers to find that wherever they might touch, there were some few Americans ready to welcome them as the representatives of the flag they all so unselfishly loved, and of the land they still so proudly called "home." Carroll, turning his wine-glass slowly between his fingers, raised his eyes to catch Holcombe's, and winked at him from behind the curtain of the smoke of his cigar, and Holcombe smiled grimly, and winked back, with the result that Meakim, who had intercepted the signalling, choked on his champagne, and had to be pounded violently on the back. Holcombe's breakfast established him as a man of means and one who could entertain properly, and after that his society was counted upon for every hour of the day. He offered money as prizes for the ship's crew to row and swim after, he gave a purse for a cross-country pony race, open to members of the Calpe and Tangier hunts, and organized picnics and riding parties innumerable. He was forced at last to hire a soldier to drive away the beggars when he walked abroad. He found it easy to be rich in a place where he was giving over two hundred copper coins for an English shilling, and he distributed his largesses recklessly and with a lack of discrimination entirely opposed to the precepts of his organized charities at home. He found it so much more amusing to throw a handful of coppers to a crowd of fat naked children than to write a check for the Society of Suppression of Cruelty to the same beneficiaries.

"You shouldn't give those fellows money," the Consul-General once remonstrated with him; " the fact that they're blind is only a proof that they have been thieves. When they catch a man stealing here they hold his head back, and pass a hot iron in front of his eyes. That's why the lids are drawn taut that way. You shouldn't encourage them."

"Perhaps they're not *all* thieves," said the District Attorney, cheerfully, as he hit the circle around him with a handful of coppers; " but there is no doubt about it that they're all blind. Which is the more to be pitied," he asked the Consul-General, " the man who has still to be found out and who can see, or the one who has been exposed and who is blind?"

"How should he know?" said Carroll, laughing. "He's never been blind, and he still holds his job."

"I don't think that's very funny," said the Consul-General.

A week of pig-sticking came to end Holcombe's stay in Tangier, and he threw himself into it and into the freedom of its life with a zest that made even the Englishman speak of him as a good fellow. He chanced to overhear this, and stopped to consider what it meant. No one had ever called him a good fellow at home, but then his life had not offered him the chance to show what sort of a good fellow he might be, and as Judge Holcombe's son certain things had been debarred him. Here he was only the richest tourist since Farwell, the diamond smuggler from Amsterdam, had touched there in his yacht.

The week of boar-hunting was spent out-of-doors, on horseback, and in tents; the women in two wide circular ones, and the men in another, with a mess tent, which they shared in common, pitched between them. They had only one change of clothes each, one wet and one dry, and they were in the saddle from nine in the morning until late at night, when they gathered in a wide circle around the wood-fire and played banjoes and listened to stories. Holcombe grew as red as a sailor, and jumped his horse over gaping crevasses in the hard sun-baked earth as recklessly as though there were nothing in this world

so well worth sacrificing one's life for as to be
the first in at a dumb brute's death. He was on
friendly terms with them all now — with Miss
Terrill, the young girl who had been awakened
by night and told to leave Monte Carlo before
daybreak, and with Mrs. Darhah, who would answer to Lady Taunton if so addressed, and with
Andrews, the Scotch bank clerk, and Ollid the
boy officer from Gibraltar, who had found some
difficulty in making the mess account balance.
They were all his very good friends, and he was
especially courteous and attentive to Miss Terrill's wants and interests, and fixed her stirrup
and once let her pass him to charge the boar in
his place. She was a silently distant young
woman, and strangely gentle for one who had
had to leave a place, and such a place, between
days ; and her hair, which was very fine and
light, ran away from under her white helmet in
disconnected curls. At night, Holcombe used to
watch her from out of the shadow when the fire-
light lit up the circle and the tips of the palms
above them, and when the story-teller's voice was
accompanied by bursts of occasional laughter from
the dragomen in the grove beyond, and the stamp-
ing and neighing of the horses at their pickets,
and the unceasing chorus of the insect life about
them. She used to sit on one of the rugs with
her hands clasped about her knees, and with her
head resting on Mrs. Hornby's broad shoulder,
looking down into the embers of the fire, and

with the story of her life written on her girl's
face as irrevocably as though old age had set its
seal there.   Holcombe was kind to them all now,
even to Meakim, when that gentleman rode leisurely out to the camp with the mail and the
latest Paris *Herald*, which was their one bond
of union with the great outside world.

Carroll sat smoking his pipe one night, and
bending forward over the fire to get its light on
the pages of the latest copy of this paper.   Suddenly he dropped it between his knees.   " I say,
Holcombe," he cried, " here's news!   Winthrop
Allen has absconded with three hundred thousand dollars, and no one knows where."

Holcombe was sitting on the other side of the
fire, prying at the rowel of his spur with a hunt-
ing-knife.   He raised his head and laughed.
"Another good man gone wrong, hey ?" he said.

Carroll lowered the paper slowly to his knee
and stared curiously through the smoky light
to where Holcombe sat intent on the rowel of his
spur.   It apparently absorbed his entire attention, and his last remark had been an unconsciously natural one.   Carroll smiled grimly as
he folded the paper across his knee.   " Now are
the mighty fallen, indeed," he murmured.   He
told Meakim of it a few minutes later, and they
both marvelled.   " It's just as I told him, isn't it,
and he wouldn't believe me.   It's the place and
the people.   Two weeks ago he would have raged.
Why, Meakim, you know Allen—Winthrop Al-

len? He's one of Holcombe's own sort; older
than he is, but one of his own people; belongs
to the same clubs; and to the same family, I
think, and yet Harry took it just as a matter of
course, with no more interest than if I'd said
that Allen was going to be married."

Meakim gave a low, comfortable laugh of content. "It makes me smile," he chuckled, "every
time I think of him the day he came up them
stairs. He scared me half to death, he did, and
then he says, just as stiff as you please, 'If you'll
leave me alone, Mr. Meakim, I'll not trouble you.'
And now it's 'Meakim this,' and 'Meakim that,'
and 'have a drink, Meakim,' just as thick as
thieves. I have to laugh whenever I think of it
now. 'If you'll leave me alone, I'll not trouble
you, Mr. Meakim.'"

Carroll pursed his lips and looked up at the
broad expanse of purple heavens with the white
stars shining through. "It's rather a pity, too, in
a way," he said, slowly. "He was all the Public
Opinion we had, and now that he's thrown up the
part, why—"

The pig-sticking came to an end finally, and
Holcombe distinguished himself by taking his
first fall, and under romantic circumst: es. He
was in an open place, with Mrs. Carroll at the edge
of the brush to his right, and Miss Terrill guard-
ing any approach from the left. They were too
far apart to speak to one another, and sat quite
still and alert to any noise as the beaters closed in

around them. There was a sharp rustle in the
reeds, and the boar broke out of it some hundred
feet ahead of Holcombe. He went after it at a
gallop, headed it off, and ran it fairly on his spear
point as it came towards him ; but as he drew his
lance clear his horse came down, falling across
him, and for the instant knocking him breathless.
It was all over in a moment. He raised his head
to see the boar turn and charge him ; he saw where
his spear point had torn the lower lip from the
long tusks, and that the blood was pouring down
its flank. He tried to draw out his legs, but the
pony lay fairly across him, kicking and struggling,
and held him in a vise. So he closed his eyes and
covered his head with his arms, and crouched in
a heap waiting. There was the quick beat of a
pony's hoofs on the hard soil, and the rush of the
boar within a foot of his head, and when he looked
up he saw Miss Terrill twisting her pony's head
around to charge the boar again, and heard her
shout "Let me have him !" to Mrs. Carroll.

Mrs. Carroll came towards Holcombe with her
spear pointed dangerously high ; she stopped at
his side and drew in her rein sharply. "Why
don't you get up? are you hurt?" she said.
"Wait; lie still," she commanded, "or he'll tramp
on you. I'll get him off." She slipped from her
saddle and dragged Holcombe's pony to his feet.
Holcombe stood up unsteadily, pale through his
tan from the pain of the fall and the moment of
fear.

THE BOAR-HUNT

"'That *was* nasty," said Mrs. Carroll, with a quick breath. She was quite as pale as he.

Holcombe wiped the dirt from his hair and the side of his face, and looked past her to where Miss Terrill was surveying the dead boar from her saddle, while her pony reared and shied, quivering with excitement beneath her. Holcombe mounted stiffly and rode towards her. "I am very much obliged to you," he said. "If you hadn't come—"

The girl laughed shortly, and shook her head without looking at him. "Why, not at all," she interrupted, quickly. "I would have come just as fast if you hadn't been there." She turned in her saddle and looked at him frankly. "I was glad to see you go down," she said, "for it gave me the first good chance I've had. Are you hurt?"

Holcombe drew himself up stiffly, regardless of the pain in his neck and shoulder. "No, I'm all right, thank you," he answered. "At the same time," he called after her as she moved away to meet the others, "you *did* save me from being torn up, whether you like it or not."

Mrs. Carroll was looking after the girl with observant, comprehending eyes. She turned to Holcombe with a smile. "There are a few things you have still to learn, Mr. Holcombe," she said, bowing in her saddle mockingly, and dropping the point of her spear to him as an adversary does in salute. "And perhaps," she added, "it is just as well that there are."

4

Holcombe trotted after her in some concern. "I wonder what she means?" he said. "I wonder if I were rude?"

The pig-sticking ended with a long luncheon before the ride back to town, at which everything that could be eaten or drunk was put on the table, in order, as Meakim explained, that there would be less to carry back. He met Holcombe that same evening after the cavalcade had reached Tangier as the latter came down the stairs of the Albion. Holcombe was in fresh raiment and cleanly shaven, and with the radiant air of one who had had his first comfortable bath in a week.

Meakim confronted him with a smiling countenance. "Who do you think come to-night on the mail-boat?" he asked.

"I don't know. Who?"

"Winthrop Allen, with six trunks," said Meakim, with the triumphant air of one who brings important news.

"No, really now," said Holcombe, laughing. "The old hypocrite! I wonder what he'll say when he sees me. I wish I could stay over another boat, just to remind him of the last time we met. What a fraud he is! It was at the club, and he was congratulating me on my noble efforts in the cause of justice, and all that sort of thing. He said I was a public benefactor. And at that time he must have already speculated away about half of what he had stolen of other people's money. I'd like to tease him about it."

"What trial was that?" asked Meakim.

Holcombe laughed and shook his head as he moved on down the stairs. "Don't ask embarrassing questions, Meakim," he said. "It was one *you* won't forget in a hurry."

"Oh!" said Meakim, with a grin. "All right. There's some mail for you in the office."

"Thank you," said Holcombe.

A few hours later Carroll was watching the roulette wheel in the gambling-hall of the Isabella when he saw Meakim come in out of the darkness, and stand staring in the doorway, blinking at the lights and mopping his face. He had been running, and was visibly excited. Carroll crossed over to him and pushed him out into the quiet of the terrace. "What is it?" he asked.

"Have you seen Holcombe?" Meakim demanded in reply.

"Not since this afternoon. Why?"

Meakim breathed heavily, and fanned himself with his hat. "Well, he's after Winthrop Allen, that's all," he panted. "And when he finds him there's going to be a muss. The boy's gone crazy. He's not safe."

"Why? What do you mean? What's Allen done to him?"

"Nothing to him, but to a friend of his. He got a letter to-night in the mail that came with Allen. It was from his sister. She wrote him all the latest news about Allen, and give him fits

for robbing an old lady who's been kind to her.
She wanted that Holcombe should come right
back and see what could be done about it. She
didn't know, of course, that Allen was coming
here. The old lady kept a private school on Fifth
Avenue, and Allen had charge of her savings."

"What is her name?" Carroll asked.

"Field, I think. Martha Field was—"

"The dirty blackguard!" cried Carroll. He
turned sharply away and returned again to seize
Meakim's arm. "Go on," he demanded. "What
did she say?"

"You know her too, do you?" said Meakim,
shaking his head sympathetically. "Well, that's
all. She used to teach his sister. She seems to
be a sort of fashionable—"

"I know," said Carroll, roughly. "She taught
my sister. She teaches everybody's sister. She's
the sweetest, simplest old soul that ever lived.
Holcombe's dead right to be angry. She almost
lived at their house when his sister was ill."

"Tut! you don't say?" commented Meakin,
gravely. "Well, his sister's pretty near crazy
about it. He give me the letter to read. It got
me all stirred up. It was just writ in blood. She
must be a fine girl, his sister. She says this Miss
Martha's money was the last thing Allen took.
He didn't use her stuff to speculate with, but
cashed it in just before he sailed and took it with
him for spending-money. His sister says she's
too proud to take help, and she's too old to work."

"How much did he take?"

"Sixty thousand. She'd been saving for over forty years."

Carroll's mind took a sudden turn. "And Holcombe?" he demanded, eagerly. "What is he going to do? Nothing silly, I hope."

"Well, that's just it. That's why I come to find you," Meakim answered, uneasily. "I don't want him to qualify for no Criminal Stakes. I got no reason to love him either— But you know—" he ended, impotently.

"Yes, I understand," said Carroll. "That's what I meant. Confound the boy, why didn't he stay in his law courts! What did he say?"

"Oh, he just raged around. He said he'd tell Allen there was an extradition treaty that Allen didn't know about, and that if Allen didn't give him the sixty thousand he'd put it in force and make him go back and stand trial."

"Compounding a felony, is he?"

"No, nothing of the sort," said Meakim, indignantly. "There isn't any extradition treaty, so he wouldn't be doing anything wrong except lying a bit."

"Well, it's blackmail, anyway."

"What, blackmail a man like Allen? Huh! He's fair game, if there ever was any. But it won't work with him, that's what I'm afraid of. He's too cunning to be taken in by it, he is. He had good legal advice before he came here, or he wouldn't have come."

Carroll was pacing up and down the terrace. He stopped and spoke over his shoulder. "Does Holcombe think Allen has the money with him?" he asked.

"Yes, he's sure of it. That's what makes him so keen. He says Allen wouldn't dare bank it at Gibraltar, because if he ever went over there to draw on it he would get caught, so he must have brought it with him here. And he got here so late that Holcombe believes it's in Allen's rooms now, and he's like a dog that smells a rat, after it. Allen wasn't in when he went up to his room, and he's started out hunting for him, and if he don't find him I shouldn't be a bit surprised if he broke into the room and just took it."

"For God's sake!" cried Carroll. "He wouldn't do that?"

Meakim pulled and fingered at his heavy watch-chain and laughed doubtfully. "I don't know," he said. "He wouldn't have done it three months ago, but he's picked up a great deal since then—since he has been with us. He's asking for Captain Reese, too."

"What's he want with that blackguard?"

"I don't know; he didn't tell me."

"Come," said Carroll, quickly. "We must stop him." He ran lightly down the steps of the terrace to the beach, with Meakim waddling heavily after him. "He's got too much at stake, Meakim," he said, in half apology, as they tramped through the sand. "IIe mustn't spoil it. We won't let him."

IIolcombe had searched the circuit of Tangier's small extent with fruitless effort, his anger increasing momentarily and feeding on each fresh disappointment. When he had failed to find the man he sought in any place, he returned to the hotel and pushed open the door of the smoking-room as fiercely as though he meant to take those within by surprise.

"IIas Mr. Allen returned?" he demanded. "Or Captain Reese?" The attendant thought not, but he would go and see. "No," IIolcombe said, "I will look for myself." He sprang up the stairs to the third floor, and turned down a passage to a door at its farthest end. Here he stopped and knocked gently. "Reese," he called; "Reese!" There was no response to his summons, and he knocked again, with more impatience, and then cautiously turned the handle of the door, and, pushing it forward, stepped into the room. "Reese," he said, softly, "it's Holcombe. Are you here?" The room was dark except for the light from the hall, which shone dimly past him and fell upon a gun-rack hanging on the wall opposite. IIolcombe hurried towards this and ran his hands over it, and passed on quickly from that to the mantel and the tables, stumbling over chairs and riding-boots as he groped about, and tripping on the skin of some animal that lay stretched upon the floor. IIe felt his way around the entire circuit of the room, and halted near the door with an exclamation of disappointment. By this time his eyes had become accustomed to the darkness, and he noted the white surface of the bed in a far corner and ran quickly towards it, groping with his hands about the posts at its head. He closed his fingers with a quick gasp of satisfaction on a leather belt that hung from it, heavy with cartridges and a revolver that swung from its holder. Holcombe pulled this out and jerked back the lever, spinning the cylinder around under the edge of his thumb. He felt the grease of each cartridge as it passed under his nail. The revolver was loaded in each chamber, and Holcombe slipped it into the pocket of his coat and crept out of the room, closing the door softly behind him. He met no one in the hall or on the stairs, and passed on quickly to a room on the second floor. There was a light in this room which showed through the transom and under the crack at the floor, and there was a sound of some one moving about within. Holcombe knocked gently and waited.

The movement on the other side of the door ceased, and after a pause a voice asked who was there. Holcombe hesitated a second before answering, and then said, " It is a servant, sir, with a note for Mr. Allen."

At the sound of some one moving towards the door from within, Holcombe threw his shoulder against the panel and pressed forward. There

was the click of the key turning in the lock and
of the withdrawal of a bolt, and the door was
partly opened. Holcombe pushed it back with
his shoulder, and, stepping quickly inside, closed
it again behind him.

The man within, into whose presence he had
forced himself, confronted him with a look of
some alarm, which increased in surprise as he
recognized his visitor. "Why, Holcombe!" he
exclaimed. He looked past him as though ex-
pecting some one else to follow. "I thought it
was a servant," he said.

Holcombe made no answer, but surveyed the
other closely, and with a smile of content. The
man before him was of erect carriage, with white
hair and whiskers, cut after an English fashion
which left the mouth and chin clean shaven. He
was of severe and dignified appearance, and
though standing as he was in dishabille still gave
in his bearing the look of an elderly gentleman
who had lived a self-respecting, well-cared-for,
and well-ordered life. The room about him was
littered with the contents of opened trunks and
uncorded boxes. He had been interrupted in the
task of unpacking and arranging these posses-
sions, but he stepped unresentfully towards the
bed where his coat lay, and pulled it on, feeling
at the open collar of his shirt, and giving a glance
of apology towards the disorder of the apart-
ment.

"The night was so warm," he said, in explana-

tion. " I have been trying to get things to rights.
I—" He was speaking in some obvious embarrassment, and looked uncertainly towards the in-
truder for help. But Holcombe made no explanation, and gave him no greeting. " I heard in the
hotel that you were here," the other continued,
still striving to cover up the difficulty of the situation, " and I am sorry to hear that you are going
so soon." He stopped, and as Holcombe still continued smiling, drew himself up stiffly. The look
on his face hardened into one of offended dignity.

" Really, Mr. Holcombe," he said, sharply, and
with strong annoyance in his tone, " if you have
forced yourself into this room for no other purpose than to stand there and laugh, I must ask
you to leave it. You may not be conscious of it,
but your manner is offensive." He turned impatiently to the table, and began rearranging the
papers upon it. Holcombe shifted the weight of
his body as it rested against the door from one
shoulder-blade to the other and closed his hands
over the door-knob behind him.

" I had a letter to-night from home about you,
Allen," he began, comfortably. " The person who
wrote it was anxious that I should return to New
York, and set things working in the District Attorney's office in order to bring you back. It
isn't you they want so much as—"

" How dare you ?" cried the embezzler, sternly,
in the voice with which one might interrupt another in words of shocking blasphemy.

"How dare I what?" asked Holcombe.

"How dare you refer to my misfortune? You of all others—" He stopped, and looked at his visitor with flashing eyes. "I thought you a gentleman," he said, reproachfully; "I thought you a man of the world, a man who in spite of your office, official position, or, rather, on account of it, could feel and understand the—a—terrible position in which I am placed, and that you would show consideration. Instead of which," he cried, his voice rising in indignation, "you have come apparently to mock at me. If the instinct of a gentleman does not teach you to be silent, I shall have to force you to respect my feelings. You can leave the room, sir. Now, at once." He pointed with his arm at the door against which Holcombe was leaning, the fingers of his outstretched hand trembling visibly.

"Nonsense. Your misfortune! What rot!" Holcombe growled resentfully. His eyes wandered around the room as though looking for some one who might enjoy the situation with him, and then returned to Allen's face. "You mustn't talk like that to me," he said, in serious remonstrance. "A man who has robbed people who trusted him for three years, as you have done, can't afford to talk of his misfortune. You were too long about it, Allen. You had too many chances to put it back. *You've* no feelings to be hurt. Besides, if you have, I'm in a hurry, and I've not the time to consider them. Now, what I want of you is—"

"Mr. Holcombe," interrupted the other, earnestly.

"Sir," replied the visitor.

"Mr. Holcombe," began Allen, slowly, and with impressive gravity, "I do not want any words with you about this, or with any one else. I am here owing to a combination of circumstances which have led me through hopeless, endless trouble. What I have gone through with nobody knows. That is something no one but I can ever understand. But that is now at an end. I have taken refuge in flight and safety, where another might have remained and compromised and suffered; but I am a weaker brother, and— as for punishment, my own conscience, which has punished me so terribly in the past, will continue to do so in the future. I am greatly to be pitied, Mr. Holcombe, greatly to be pitied. And no one knows that better than yourself. You know the value of the position I held in New York city, and how well I was suited to it, and it to me. And now I am robbed of it all. I am an exile in this wilderness. Surely, Mr. Holcombe, this is not the place nor the time when you should insult me by recalling the—"

"You contemptible hypocrite," said Holcombe, slowly. "What an ass you must think I am! Now, listen to me."

"No, *you* listen to me," thundered the other. He stepped menacingly forward, his chest heaving under his open shirt, and his fingers opening

and closing at his side. "Leave the room, I tell
you," he cried, "or I shall call the servants and
make you!" He paused with a short, mocking
laugh. "Who do you think I am?" he asked;
"a child that you can insult and jibe at? I'm
not a prisoner in the box for you to browbeat
and bully, Mr. District Attorney. You seem to
forget that I am out of your jurisdiction now."

He waited, and his manner seemed to invite
Holcombe to make some angry answer to his
tone, but the young man remained grimly silent.

"You are a very important young person at
home, Harry," Allen went on, mockingly. "But
New York State laws do not reach as far as
Africa."

"Quite right; that's it exactly," said Holcombe, with cheerful alacrity. "I'm glad you
have grasped the situation so soon. That makes
it easier for me. Now, what I have been trying
to tell you is this. I received a letter about you
to-night. It seems that before leaving New York
you converted bonds and mortgages belonging to
Miss Martha Field, which she had intrusted to
you, into ready money. And that you took this
money with you. Now, as this is the first place
you have stopped since leaving New York, except
Gibraltar, where you could not have banked it,
you must have it with you now, here in this
town, in this hotel, possibly in this room. What
else you have belonging to other poor devils and
corporations does not concern me. It's yours as

far as I mean to do anything about it. But this sixty thousand dollars which belongs to Miss Field, who is the best, purest, and kindest woman I have ever known, and who has given away more money than you ever stole, is going back with me to-morrow to New York." Holcombe leaned forward as he spoke, and rapped with his knuckles on the table. Allen confronted him in amazement, in which there was not so much surprise at what the other threatened to do as at the fact that it was he who had proposed doing it.

"I don't understand," he said, slowly, with the air of a bewildered child.

"It's plain enough," replied the other, impatiently. "I tell you I want sixty thousand dollars of the money you have with you. You can understand that, can't you?"

"But how?" expostulated Allen. "You don't mean to rob me, do you, Harry?" he asked, with a laugh.

"You're a very stupid person for so clever a one," Holcombe said, impatiently. "You must give me sixty thousand dollars—and if you don't, I'll take it. Come, now, where is it—in that box?" He pointed with his finger towards a square travelling-case covered with black leather that stood open on the table filled with papers and blue envelopes.

"Take it!" exclaimed Allen. "You, Henry Holcombe? Is it you who are speaking? Do I hear you?" He looked at Holcombe with eyes full of genuine wonder and a touch of fear. As he spoke his hand reached out mechanically and drew the leather-bound box towards him.

"Ah, it is in that box, then," said Holcombe, in a quiet, grave tone. "Now count it out, and be quick."

"Are you drunk?" cried the other, fiercely. "Do you propose to turn highwayman and thief? What do you mean?" Holcombe reached quickly across the table towards the box, but the other drew it back, snapping the lid down, and hugging it close against his breast. "If you move, Holcombe," he cried, in a voice of terror and warning, "I'll call the people of the house and — and expose you."

"Expose me, you idiot," returned Helcombe, fiercely. "How dare *you* talk to *me* like that!"

Allen dragged the table more evenly between them, as a general works on his defences even while he parleys with the enemy. "It's you who are the idiot!" he cried. "Suppose you could overcome me, which would be harder than you think, what are you going to do with the money? Do you suppose I'd let you leave this country with it? Do you imagine for a moment that I would give it up without raising my hand? I'd have you dragged to prison from your bed this very night, or I'd have you seized as you set your foot upon the wharf. I would appeal to our Consul-General. As far as he knows, I am as worthy of protection as you are yourself, and, failing him, I'd appeal to the law of the land." He stopped for want of breath, and then began again with the air of one who finds encouragement in the sound of his own voice. "They may not understand extradition here, Holcombe," he said, "but a thief is a thief all the world over. What you may be in New York isn't going to help you here ; neither is your father's name. To these people you would be only a hotel thief who forces his way into other men's rooms at night and—"

"You poor thing," interrupted Holcombe. "Do you know where you are?" he demanded. "You talk, Allen, as though we were within sound of the cable-cars on Broadway. This hotel is not the Brunswick, and this Consul-General you speak of is another blackguard who knows that a word from me at Washington, on my return, or a letter from here would lose him his place and his liberty. He's as much of a rascal as any of them, and he knows that I know it and that I may use that knowledge. *He* won't help you. And as for the law of the land"—Holcombe's voice rose and broke in a mocking laugh —"there is no law of the land. *That's why you're here!* You are in a place populated by exiles and outlaws like yourself, who have preyed upon society until society has turned and frightened each of them off like a dog with his tail between his legs. Don't give yourself confidence, Allen. That's all you are, that's all we are—two dogs fighting for a stolen bone. The man who rules

you here is an ignorant negro, debauched and
vicious and a fanatic. He is shut off from every
one, even to the approach of a British ambassador.
And what do you suppose he cares for a dog
of a Christian like you, who has been robbed in
a hotel by another Christian? And these others.
Do you suppose they care? Call out — cry for
help, and tell them that you have half a million
dollars in this room, and they will fall on you
and strip you of every cent of it, and leave you
to walk the beach for work. Now, what are you
going to do? Will you give me the money I
want to take back where it belongs, or will you
call for help and lose it all?"

The two men confronted each other across the
narrow length of the table. The blood had run
to Holcombe's face, but the face of the other was
drawn and pale with fear.

"You can't frighten me," he gasped, rallying
his courage with an effort of the will. "You are
talking nonsense. This is a respectable hotel; it
isn't a den of thieves. You are trying to frighten
me out of the money with your lies and your
lawyer's tricks, but you will find that I am not so
easily fooled. You are dealing with a man, Holcombe, who suffered to get what he has, and who
doesn't mean to let it go without a fight for it.
Come near me, I warn you, and I shall call for
help."

Holcombe backed slowly away from the table
and tossed up his hands with the gesture of one

5

who gives up his argument. "You will have it, will you?" he muttered, grimly. "Very well, you *shall* fight for it." He turned quickly and drove in the bolt of the door and placed his shoulders over the electric button in the wall. "I have warned you," he said, softly. "I have told you where you are, and that you have nothing to expect from the outside. You are absolutely in my power to do with as I please." He stopped, and, without moving his eyes from Allen's face, drew the revolver from the pocket of his coat. His manner was so terrible that Allen gazed at him, breathing faintly, and with his eyes fixed in horrible fascination. "There is no law," Holcombe repeated, softly. "There is no help for you now or later. It is a question of two men locked in a room with a table and sixty thousand dollars between them. That is the situation. Two men and sixty thousand dollars. We have returned to first principles, Allen. It is a man against a man, and there is no Court of Appeal."

Allen's breath came back to him with a gasp, as though he had been shocked with a sudden downpour of icy water.

"There is!" he cried. "There *is* a Court of Appeal. For God's sake, wait. I appeal to Henry Holcombe, to Judge Holcombe's son. I appeal to your good name, Harry, to your fame in the world. Think what you are doing; for the love of God, don't murder me. I'm a criminal, I know, but not what you would be, Holcombe; not that.

You are mad or drunk. You wouldn't, you couldn't do it. Think of it! *You*, Henry Holcombe. *You*."

The fingers of Holcombe's hand moved and tightened around the butt of the pistol, the sweat sprang from the pores of his palm. He raised the revolver and pointed it. "My sin's on my own head," he said. "Give me the money."

The older man glanced fearfully back of him at the open window, through which a sea breeze moved the palms outside, so that they seemed to whisper together as though aghast at the scene before them. The window was three stories from the ground, and Allen's eyes returned to the stern face of the younger man. As they stood silent there came to them the sound of some one moving in the hall, and of men's voices whispering together. Allen's face lit with a sudden radiance of hope, and Holcombe's arm moved uncertainly.

"I fancy," he said, in a whisper, "that those are my friends. They have some idea of my purpose, and they have come to learn more. If you call, I will let them in, and they will strangle you into silence until I get the money."

The two men eyed each other steadily, the older seeming to weigh the possible truth of Holcombe's last words in his mind. Holcombe broke the silence in a lighter tone.

"Playing the policeman is a new rôle to me," he said, "and I warn you that I have but little patience ; and, besides, my hand is getting tired, and this thing is at full cock."

Allen, for the first time, lowered the box upon the table and drew from it a bundle of notes bound together with elastic bandages. Holcombe's eyes lighted as brightly at the sight as though the notes were for his own private pleasures in the future.

"Be quick!" he said. "I cannot be responsible for the men outside."

Allen bent over the money, his face drawing into closer and sharper lines as the amount grew, under his fingers, to the sum Holcombe had demanded.

"Sixty thousand!" he said, in a voice of desperate calm.

"Good!" whispered Holcombe. "Pass it over to me. I hope I have taken the most of what you have," he said, as he shoved the notes into his pocket; "but this is something. Now I warn you," he added, as he lowered the trigger of the revolver and put it out of sight, "that any attempt to regain this will be futile. I am surrounded by friends; no one knows you or cares about you. I shall sleep in my room to-night without precaution, for I know that the money is now mine. Nothing you can do will recall it. Your cue is silence and secrecy as to what you have lost and as to what you still have with you."

He stopped in some confusion, interrupted by a sharp knock at the door and two voices calling his name. Allen shrank back in terror.

"You coward!" he hissed. "You promised me you'd be content with what you have." Holcombe looked at him in amazement. "And now your accomplices are to have their share, too, are they?" the embezzler whispered, fiercely. "You lied to me; you mean to take it all."

Holcombe, for an answer, drew back the bolt, but so softly that the sound of his voice drowned the noise it made.

"No, not to-night," he said, briskly, so that the sound of his voice penetrated into the hall beyond. "I mustn't stop any longer, I'm keeping you up. It has been very pleasant to have heard all that news from home. It was such a chance, my seeing you before I sailed. Good-night." He paused and pretended to listen. "No, Allen, I don't think it's a servant," he said. "It's some of my friends looking for me. This is my last night on shore, you see." He threw open the door and confronted Meakim and Carroll as they stood in some confusion in the dark hall. "Yes, it is some of my friends," Holcombe continued. "I'll be with you in a minute," he said to them. Then he turned, and, crossing the room in their sight, shook Allen by the hand, and bade him good-night and good-bye.

The embezzler's revulsion of feeling was so keen and the relief so great that he was able to smile as Holcombe turned and left him. "I wish you a pleasant voyage," he said, faintly.

Then Holcombe shut the door on him, closing him out from their sight. He placed his hands on a shoulder of each of the two men, and jumped step by step down the stairs like a boy as they descended silently in front of him. At the foot of the stairs Carroll turned and confronted him sternly, staring him in the face. Meakim at one side eyed him curiously.

" Well ?" said Carroll, with one hand upon Holcombe's wrist.

Holcombe shook his hand free, laughing. "Well," he answered, "I persuaded him to make restitution."

"You persuaded him !" exclaimed Carroll, impatiently. "How ?"

Holcombe's eyes avoided those of the two inquisitors. He drew a long breath, and then burst into a loud fit of hysterical laughter. The two men surveyed him grimly. "I argued with him, of course," said Holcombe, gayly. "That is my business, man ; you forget that I am a District Attorney—"

"*We* didn't forget it," said Carroll, fiercely. "Did *you?* What did you do?"

Holcombe backed away up the stairs shaking his head and laughing. "I shall never tell you," he said. He pointed with his hand down the second flight of stairs. "Meet me in the smoking-room," he continued. "I will be there in a minute, and we will have a banquet. Ask the others to come. I have something to do first."

The two men turned reluctantly away, and continued on down the stairs without speaking and with their faces filled with doubt. Holcombe ran first to Reese's room and replaced the pistol in its holder. He was trembling as he threw the thing from him, and had barely reached his own room and closed the door when a sudden faintness overcame him. The weight he had laid on his nerves was gone and the laughter had departed from his face. He stood looking back at what he had escaped as a man reprieved at the steps of the gallows turns his head to glance at the rope he has cheated. Holcombe tossed the bundle of notes upon the table and took an unsteady step across the room. Then he turned suddenly and threw himself upon his knees and buried his face in the pillow.

The sun rose the next morning on a cool, beautiful day, and the consul's boat, with the American flag trailing from the stern, rose and fell on the bluest of blue waters as it carried Holcombe and his friends to the steamer's side.

"We are going to miss you very much," Mrs. Carroll said. "I hope you won't forget to send us word of yourself."

Miss Terrill said nothing. She was leaning over the side trailing her hand in the water, and watching it run between her slim pink fingers. She raised her eyes to find Holcombe looking at her intently with a strange expression of wistfulness and pity, at which she smiled brightly back at him, and began to plan vivaciously with Captain Reese for a ride that same afternoon.

They separated over the steamer's deck, and

Meakim, for the hundredth time, and in the lack of conversation which comes at such moments, offered Holcombe a fresh cigar.

"But I have got eight of yours now," said Holcombe.

"That's all right ; put it in your pocket," said the Tammany chieftain, "and smoke it after dinner. You'll need 'em. They're better than those you'll get on the steamer, and they never went through a custom-house."

Holcombe cleared his throat in some slight embarrassment. "Is there anything I can do for you in New York, Meakim?" he asked. "Anybody I can see, or to whom I can deliver a message ?"

"No," said Meakim. "I write pretty often. Don't you worry about me," he added, gratefully. "I'll be back there some day myself, when the law of limitation lets me."

Holcombe laughed. "Well," he said, "I'd be glad to do something for you if you'd let me know what you'd like."

Meakim put his hands behind his back and puffed meditatively on his cigar, rolling it between his lips with his tongue. Then he turned it between his fingers and tossed the ashes over the side of the boat. He gave a little sigh, and then frowned at having done so. "I'll tell you what you *can* do for me, Holcombe," he said, smiling. "Some night I wish you would go down to Fourteenth Street, some night this spring, when

the boys are sitting out on the steps in front of
the Hall, and just take a drink for me at Ed Lal-
ly's; just for luck. Will you? That's what I'd
like to do. I don't know nothing better than
Fourteenth Street of a summer evening, with all
the people crowding into Pastor's on one side of
the Hall, and the Third Avenue L cars running
by on the other. That's a gay sight; ain't it now?
With all the girls coming in and out of Theiss's,
and the sidewalks crowded. One of them warm
nights when they have to have the windows open,
and you can hear the music in at Pastor's, and the
audience clapping their hands. That's great, isn't
it? Well," he laughed and shook his head. "I'll
be back there some day, won't I," he said, wist-
fully, "and hear it for myself."

"Carroll," said Holcombe, drawing the former
to one side, "suppose I see this cabman when I
reach home, and get him to withdraw the charge,
or agree not to turn up when it comes to trial."

Carroll's face clouded in an instant. "Now,
listen to me, Holcombe," he said. "You let my
dirty work alone. There's lots of my friends who
have nothing better to do than just that. You
have something better to do, and you leave me
and my rows to others. I like you for what you
are, and not for what you can do for me. I don't
mean that I don't appreciate your offer, but it
shouldn't have come from an Assistant District
Attorney to a fugitive criminal."

"What nonsense!" said Holcombe.

"Don't say that; don't say that!" said Carroll, quickly, as though it hurt him. "You wouldn't have said it a month ago."

Holcombe eyed the other with an alert, confident smile. "No, Carroll," he answered, "I would not." He put his hand on the other's shoulder with a suggestion in his manner of his former self, and with a touch of patronage. "I have learned a great deal in a month," he said. "Seven battles were won in seven days once. All my life I have been fighting causes, Carroll, and principles. I have been working with laws against law-breakers. I have never yet fought a man. It was not poor old Meakim, the individual, I prosecuted, but the corrupt politician. Now, here I have been thrown with men and women on as equal terms as a crew of sailors cast away upon a desert island. We were each a law unto himself. And I have been brought face to face, and for the first time in my life, not with principles of conduct, not with causes, and not with laws, but with my fellow-men."

THE WRITING ON THE WALL

IMMEN PASHA's dinner was given to Miss Page, although it was ostensibly in honor of the British Minister, whose wife sat on Immen's right, and tested that Oriental's composed politeness greatly. But at times he would turn to Miss Page, and she would murmur with him in French, and he would have his reward. The condition upon which Miss Page had come to the dinner was that it should be an Oriental one throughout, and so the table was accordingly of silver, and each strange, sticky course was served in a golden bowl, and each fork and spoon bore a ruby and a diamond in its handle.

"Diamonds and rubies are my jewels," Immen explained simply, as one would say, "Blue and yellow are my racing colors," or that such a sentence was the motto of his family.

A native orchestra played from a balcony of heavily carved wood that stretched across one end of the room, and behind a lattice beneath it shone the bright eyes of Immen's wife, who was politely supposed to have already departed for Alexandria, but who in reality was looking with wonder and misgivings upon the bold women, with naked faces and shoulders, who sat at her husband's side, and talked to him without waiting for him to give them leave.

Miss Page and her family had been spending the winter in Cairo, and were to leave in the week. The hot weather, or what passes for hot weather in Cairo, had arrived, and the last of Cook's dahabeahs was hurrying back down the Nile, and a few of the court had already gone to Alexandria, and in two weeks the Khedive would follow. It had been a delightful winter, and Helen Page had enjoyed it in what was to her a new way. She had reached that stage when everything in life has found its true value. There was for her no more marking up or marking down. If it would not sell for that it should not leave her, or if it cost so much it was not worth seeking after, and she let it go. She still enjoyed dances and functions; but the dances had to be very well done, and the functions had to come in the natural order of things. She knew what bored her and what amused her, and she knew the worth of a cabinet minister's conversation and the value of a few words from royalty, and of a day with her brother hunting for bargains in the bazaars. She had arrived.

She left the officers of the Army of Occupation to her sister, who was just out, and of that age when the man who leads the cotillon was of much more immediate importance than the gentleman with the star on his coat, who could tell her sister when the Italians would move over the Alps, or the tall senators in Washington who related such amusing stories and who told things to Helen of such importance that she would sit with her eyes cast down so that people might not see how interested she was. That might be worth while to Helen, but to her sister the young English officers on polo ponies and the rides to the ostrich farm and golf at the base of the pyramids were much more entertaining. So it happened occasionally when Helen and her good-looking brother were treasure-hunting on the Mouski that they would have to jump out of the way of a yelling outrunner in black and gold and see their sister roll by seated high in a cart with an Arabian pony in the shafts and an English subaltern at her side.

Once when this happened her brother looked after the cart with a smile, and said, indulgently and with that tolerance for youth which only a Harvard Junior can feel:

"Wouldn't you like to be as young as that, Helen?"

His sister exclaimed, indignantly: "Well, upon my word! And how old do you suppose I am?"

"I don't know," the brother answered, unabashed. "The last time I asked you, you were nineteen. That was years ago."

"Only four years. Does that make me so very old?"

"But you've seen such a lot, and you've been around so much and all that," he argued. "That's what makes people old. Helen, don't you ever intend to get married?"

"Never," said the sister. "I am going to live with you, and keep you from falling in love with a nicer girl than myself, and we will promise each other never to marry, but just to go about like this always, and explore places and have adventures."

Young Page laughed indulgently. "Very well," he said. He had had hopes at one time that his sister would take a fancy to his room-mate, who played next to him on the foot-ball eleven; but that gentleman had never really appreciated her, although he had once said that her photograph was the finest thing he had ever seen. He used to stand in front of it when he was filling his pipe and survey it critically, with his head on one side, and Page had considered this a very good sign. It was after this that the announcement in the papers of his sister's engagement to a young English duke had made her brother wonder if that perhaps would not be even a better thing for him, as it would give him such grand opportunities for shooting over his brother-in-law's preserves. And from that time on he rather discouraged his room-mate in cherishing secret hopes.

He had not heard of the young Englishman lately, so he inquired, jocosely and with what he considered rare discretion and subtlety: "If you

were to marry a duke, Helen, should I still call
you just plain Helen, or would you make me say
'Your Grace,' as the servants do?"

Helen stopped, ankle-deep in the mud of the bazaars, and surveyed him with such evident amusement that he laughed in some embarrassment.
"You could never truthfully call me 'plain Helen,'
Ted," she said, "and you will never have the
chance to call me the other thing."

"Oh!" said her brother, meekly, "that's how
it is, is it?"

"Yes, that's how it is," his sister echoed him.

The man who sat on Miss Page's left at Immen
Pasha's dinner was Prince Panine, the Russian
First Secretary.   He had known Miss Page in
Washington when he was an attaché of the Russian legation there, and had been bold enough to
ask her to marry him.   When she declined to do
so, he took it hardly, and said unpleasant things
about her, which, in time, came back to her.   She
bore him no ill-will for this; but he did not appeal to her as a delightful dinner companion.
It was different with the Russian, for it was his
pride that had been hurt by her refusal rather
than his heart, and he thought this the sweet
moment of his revenge.   He now could show
the woman who had refused him when he was
an insignificant attaché that it was the prospec-
tive head of a powerful and noble Russian family and a possible ambassador that she had over-
looked.

He felt the value of the situation keenly. It inspired him as a good part inspires the actor, and he smiled at his own thoughts, and twisted his pointed beard, and bridled and bowed his head like a pretty woman. Miss Page at first did not notice him at all. She was intent on what Immen was telling her of some extravagance of Ismaïl Pasha's, in whose cabinet he had served; but when he had ceased, and turned with a sigh to the English matron, Miss Page moved in her chair, and surveyed Panine with smiling good-nature.

"It is very nice to see you again," she said, comfortably; "but they tell me, Prince, that you are such a dangerous personage now. I am really rather afraid of you."

The Russian bowed his head and smiled grimly. "You did not find me dangerous once," he said.

But she looked past him, and continued as though he had not spoken. "I never thought you would take the service so seriously," she went on. "Why, you will be a minister very soon now, shall you not?"

Panine looked at her sternly, as though he was in doubt as to her being serious. "Some one has told you?" he asked, frowning.

"No," she said, lightly. "But it is about time, is it not? What were you in Washington? Second Secretary, I think?"

"It is not a matter of years," the Russian an-

swered, stiffly—"at least, it is not so with some
men. It is true I am still a secretary, but our
chief has been away, and—what is it that you
have for a proverb—'when the cat's away the
mice'—eh?" He lifted his eyebrows, and then
glanced quickly up and down the length of the
table, as though to give her the impression that
he was fearful of having been overheard. Miss
Page did not apparently notice this by-play. She
laughed, and then interrupted herself to listen to
something that was being said across the table
before she answered him.

"So," she said, "you have been plotting and
conspiring again, have you, and we are to have a
crisis? You are all just alike." She laughed indulgently. "It is so absurd," she said.

Panine's frown was quite genuine now. "Ah,
so," he said, with mocking politeness, "you think
it absurd? Yes," he added, "you are quite right.
It is nothing, just a game, and, as you say, quite
absurd—quite absurd. You relieve me," he added.
"I had feared perhaps you had learned something. Even the most experienced in our service
is sometimes indiscreet, when it is a beautiful
woman to whom he talks."

Her eyes closed for an instant, which was a
trick they had when she was annoyed or bored,
and she turned to Immen with a smile. The Russian sipped deeply from his glass and scowled.
He felt that he was not making that sort of an
impression which the situation should have called

forth. The girl did not yet seem to appreciate what she had given up.

Miss Page turned to him again. "We are to have a most amusing evening," she said; "did you know? Immen is going to have Bannerman in to do his tricks for us."

"The mind-reader?"

"Yes. Have you ever seen him?"

Panine answered, in the tone of one who is tolerant of the amusements of others, that he had seen the fellow once when he had performed before the King of Greece. "He made us all look rather ridiculous and undignified," he said. "I do not think that I like the court jester of modern times."

"You must be very careful," Miss Page laughed, "or he will read all of your secrets, and then we will know what mischief you have been—"

"I beg your pardon!" interrupted the Russian, quickly. He gave her a warning glance. "They will hear you," he explained.

The girl tossed her head with a shrug of impatience. "Quelle pose!" she said. "Why are you not amusing, as you used to be? Are you always mysterious now? And when are you Russians going to embrace France, and how soon will your fleet be in the Bosporus, and do you still draw little maps of Constantinople on the backs of your visiting-cards? Oh, it is such an old, old story."

"Just as you say," replied Panine, without

showing any sense of injury. "It is an old story; it is like the shepherd-boy who kept calling that the wolf was coming, is it not?"

"Exactly," consented the girl, "except that the Russian specimen of wolf never comes."

Panine smiled and nodded his head. "Do you know something, Miss Page?" he said. "You should have been in a secret service. You should have been a diplomat."

"I don't think I like that," said the girl, slowly, "though you probably meant that I should. Why?"

"Because the methods you adopt in finding out what you wish to know are the ones which will make you sure to learn. Make little of another's secret, Miss Page, or of another's knowledge, and he is sure to tell you what he knows, because he is piqued and wishes to show you how important it is or how important he is."

"My dear Prince," said the girl, patiently, "I have not the *least* desire to know your secrets. I have no 'methods.' I am quite innocent of trying to find out anything. You do yourself entirely too much honor. Even if you had a secret, it would make me most uncomfortable if I thought you had it about you, and especially if I imagined you intended to let it escape."

"You treat me this way," said the Russian, quickly, and lowering his voice, "because you still even now look at me as a boy. You think that I have been doing nothing these five years; that I am still copying despatches and translating reports. But that is past. I send despatches myself now, and in a short time my government and every government will know that I have not been idle. What I am doing now will be the talk of the whole diplomatic world."

The man leaned forward and poured out his words in a low and intense whisper. He was mortified, and his pride cut to the heart at the coldness of the woman beside him. Had she begged for his confidence he could have withheld it easily, as his caution would have taken alarm at her entreaties ; but her silent indifference to him and to what he knew was of momentous importance piqued and unnerved him. He was sure she was discreet ; it was the one quality that every man and woman unhesitatingly allowed to her ;· and more than that, she was very beautiful. A man will tell a discreet woman a great deal, and when she has added to this virtue great beauty, he is liable to tell her everything, unless she stops him.

" There are those here at this table," continued Panine, with his eyes bent on his plate, " who are in danger. In a week, in a day, the crisis at which you laugh will come, and some of those who are here to-night will not dine with us again."

Miss Page considered that it was now quite time for him to stop. " I had no idea you were serious," she said, haughtily. "Who gave you the right to confide in me?"

She turned for relief to Immen, but he was deep in conversation with his neighbor, so she became silent, and interested herself in the dish before her. "Do you know what this is?" she asked Panine, in a lighter tone. "I have been studying very hard since I have been here, but I never seem to learn the names of anything useful."

Panine was biting at his finger-nail. He had worked himself up into a fever of excitement. For months his thoughts had been on one theme, and in working out what was to be for him a great *coup*, which was to place him at the head of a legation and cover his coat with French and Russian orders. He could think of nothing else, and he could not now contain himself.

"You know the situation here," he went on, anxiously, as though she had not previously checked him. "It is three to one, if you went less with your English friends, and saw more of *us*, you would feel less confident, you would have less of their arrogance and intolerance of the enemy. It is not wise to despise an enemy. What would you think if the Dual Control, which is not a Dual Control, should be revived, but with this important difference, that it shall be France and Russia, and not France and England, who are to guide the future of these Egyptians?"

Miss Page glanced with a smile down the table to where the English Consul-General sat, large, broad - shouldered, and aggressive - looking even over his sweetmeats. He caught her eye, and smiled pleasantly.

"That is not a very thrilling idea," she said. "It seems to me it has been in the air for some time. Not that I follow politics at all," she added, quickly, "but every one knows that; it is certainly not new."

"The idea, no; but the carrying out of it, yes," said the Russian. He leaned forward and towards her quickly, and before she could draw her head away had whispered to her a few words in English, which was the safest tongue he could have used in that company. Then he drew back, his eyes brilliant with triumph and excitement, and noted the effect of his words.

The girl's face had paled, and her eyes were wide open, as though she had seen something that shocked her, and she even made a movement as though she would push back her chair and leave the table. But as the color came to her cheeks her self - possession returned to her, and she bent her body forward and said across the table to one of the English women opposite:

"I hear you are going to sail with us next week. That will be very nice. I hope it will be smooth between here and Brindisi."

Panine exclaimed under his breath, and whispered something between his fingers as he twisted them in his pointed beard.

There were many people at the reception which followed the dinner; wise-looking judges of the Mixed Courts and their wives and native princes, secretaries of the many diplomatic agencies, and an abundance of scarlet mess jackets on officers of the Army of Occupation. They outshone even the women in the brilliancy of their apparel, with their broad bands of gold braid and rows of tiny brass buttons. They outshone the men, too, in the ruddy tan of their faces, burned by the sun of the Soudan and roughened by the fine sand of the desert.

They were a handsome, arrogant-looking group; some with the fez, which seemed strangely out of place on their yellow hair, and which showed that they served the Khedive, and others with strips of tiny ribbons across their breasts to show that they had served the Queen, and each of these Englishmen moved about with the uneasy, self-assertive air of one who knows that he is welcomed through necessity, and only because he holds his place in the society about him by force of arms.

Bannerman, the English mind-reader, busied himself in selecting a committee, and the others seated themselves on the divans around the room and discussed the self-possessed young woman with the yellow-dyed hair who served as the mind-reader's assistant, and to whom he referred as "my ward." They all agreed that he was certainly very clever, and as an entertainer a decided relief after the amateur musicians of doubtful talent who had been forced upon them at other houses.

Bannerman showed how some one else had stabbed the Austrian Minister in the back with a paper-knife, after first having discovered it hidden in a pot of palms in the garden. And his assistant, at his command, described rings and coins and pocket-pieces held up before her blindfolded eyes. Then Bannerman read the numbers on an English bank-note, chalking them out on a blackboard, and rearranged groups and tableaux which had been previously stage-managed and separated during his absence from the room. He was extremely easy and clever, and smiled an offensively humble smile as each exhibition was rewarded by enthusiastic approbation. Nothing quite so out of the common had been given them during the season. Magicians they had in plenty; they could be found on the terrace of Shepheard's any afternoon, but there was something almost uncanny in the successes of this English adventurer, which was slightly spoiled by his self-assurance, by the rows of medals on his coat, and the barbarous jewels on his short, fat fingers.

Hoffmeyer Bey, a German in the Egyptian service, took it very seriously.

"I should like to ask you, sir," he demanded,

as though the mind-reader were on trial, and gazing at him grimly through round spectacles, "whether you claim to *will* the young lady to say what these articles are which you hold up, or whether you claim to communicate with her by thought-transference."

Some of the subalterns nudged each other and grinned at this. They did not know how the trick was done, but they did know that it was a trick. You could not impose on them.

"I should answer that, sir, in this way," said the showman, glibly: "I should say that it is an exhibition of *both* will-power and of thought-transference. You observe, ladies and gentlemen, that I do not even approach my assistant, so that it is not muscle-reading I depend upon, which is a very different thing from mind-reading, and which necessitates actual contact. I see whatever it is that you wish described. My mind is working in sympathy with my ward's, and I will her to tell of what I am thinking. If I did not keep my mind on the object, she could give no description of it whatsoever."

Colonel Royce raised his finger. "Eh—could she give a description of it if you merely thought of it, but didn't say anything?" he demanded.

Miss Page, who was sitting at Immen's side in a far corner, smiled and shrugged her shoulders.

"Why don't they let the poor man alone?" she said. "It is a very good trick, and is all the more

amusing because we think it is not a trick. Why
insist on seeing the wheels go round?"

"Oh, he will explain," said the old Pasha, smiling. "C'est son métier. He has been asked these
same questions before. He is quite prepared for
them, and in a contest of argument I imagine the
fakir would be more than a match for our military friend. The colonel, they tell me, is more
at home in a saddle than in a salon."

"The best test I could possibly submit to you,"
said Bannerman, "and one which would show you
that there is no collusion between myself and my
assistant, is one that I call 'The writing on the
wall.' I will take any one you please to select as
my subject, and make him or her write a sentence
on this blackboard in a language which he or she
does not understand. I will not dictate what the
subject writes. I simply claim to be able to make
him write it in a language which he does not know.
If I can do this, you must admit that I have the
power to will another to read what is in my mind,
just as I am able to read what is in his mind. I
think that is the just conclusion. I act in the
test simply as a translator. The subject thinks
of a sentence or phrase, and I translate it in my
own mind, and force him by will-power alone to
write it in a language with which he is absolutely
unfamiliar. All I ask is that I may be allowed to
blindfold whoever assists me in this, in order that
he may not have his attention distracted, and to
be allowed to hold his hand."

"Will you please say that all over again?" commanded Colonel Royce.

Bannerman explained his test once more, and there was a general murmur of incredulity and of whispered persiflage on the part of the subalterns.

"If he can make you write three words in correct French, Ted," said his younger sister, "I'll believe he's a spook."

The English Minister turned to his American confrère with a smile. "That sounds rather interesting," he said. "How will he do it?"

The American was sitting with his lips puckered and with his eyes half closed. "I was just trying to think," he said, doubtfully. "Of course it is a trick. I don't believe in thought transference myself. He either moves his assistant's hand, and makes him think that he is doing it himself when he is not, or the assistant does what the little boy did. There is no other way."

"What did the little boy do? Is that an American story?" said the Englishman, smiling.

"Oh, the little boy lied," explained the Consul-General.

Bannerman stood in the centre of the room, weighing a broad silk scarf in his hands. "There is too much light for my purpose," he said; "it prevents my concentrating my thoughts. Would you mind having two or three of those lamps placed outside, if you please? Thank you."

The lamps were carried out, and the room was

now left in an appropriate half-light, which came mysteriously from under red globes. There was an interested silence.

Bannerman stood weighing the handkerchief in the palms of his hands and glancing slowly around the surrounding rows of faces. His eyes rested finally on the farther corner, where Helen Page sat in an alcove with the English woman who was to sail with her the week following. They were whispering together busily, and Immen Pasha had turned his shoulder to them so that they might speak the more freely. Bannerman walked directly towards them without speaking or making any sound, but as he came forward Miss Page turned her head sharply, and looked at him inquiringly as though he had already addressed her. He stood immediately before her and bowed.

"Will you be so good as to assist me in this?" he asked. He bowed again, smiling as he did so, with so assured an air that Immen rose and placed himself between them.

"No," he answered for her. "You must ask some one else."

"I should be very much gratified if this young lady would assist me," said the adventurer, earnestly, but in so low a tone that those at the other end of the room could hear nothing. "I am quite confident I could succeed with her. It is a most difficult experiment."

Miss Page shook her head slightly. "Thank you, no," she said.

She turned to her friend and began speaking
with her again as though nothing had interrupted
them. The mind-reader made no second effort to
address her, neither did he move away, but stood
perfectly still, looking at her curiously and fixed-
ly. The girl stopped as though some one had
touched her to attract her attention, and, looking
up, met the eyes of the mind-reader fixed upon
hers. The man took courage from the silence in
the room, which showed him that his choice had
been a popular one, and that the girl whose money
and beauty and brains had in their different fashion interested different people was a personage of
whom they wished to see more in a new part. Even
Immen himself stood aside now ; he, too, was curious to see how she would acquit herself.

"Come," said the man, in a low tone. The girl
stared at him in surprise and drew back.

She turned to Immen. "What does he want
with me ?" she said.

"It is nothing, madam," answered Bannerman,
quickly, before the older man could speak to her ;
"merely to write a sentence on the blackboard.
Anything that comes into your head, and I shall
will you to write it in any language I please."

The girl's face wore a troubled, puzzled look,
and instead of turning her eyes away, she continued staring at the man as though she were trying
to recollect whether she had ever seen him before.

He drew away from her slowly, and with his
eyes still fixed on hers. "You will assist me," he

said. And this time it was not in a tone of inquiry that he spoke, but of command.

The girl rose suddenly, and stood uncertainly,
looking around the room as though to test its feeling towards her. She saw the English Minister
(as that Consul-General was called by courtesy)
smiling at her encouragingly, she saw Panine in a
doorway, posed against the red curtains, scowling
to himself, and she saw her brother and sister,
surrounded by a full staff of scarlet jackets, en-
joying her discomfiture. She took a step back as
though to resume her place in the alcove, but the
mind-reader put out his hand, and she, to the surprise of all, took it, staring at him as she did so,
as though to read in his face how he had been able
to make her give it to him.

" You understand French, of course," the man
said, in a low tone, but the room was so still now
that every one could hear. The girl nodded,
without taking her eyes from his. " And Italian
—yes ; and German—yes ; and a little Spanish—
perhaps—yes—no ? Is that all ?" The girl nodded
again.

" Very good. You shall write in Arabic."

The Egyptians and the English looked at each
other and smiled, but the tone of the man was so
full of confidence that their faces filled again with
intent interest. Carefully and deftly Bannerman
drew the silk scarf across the girl's forehead, but
she raised her hands and unwound it and dropped
it on the floor.

"I will not be blindfolded," she said. "I can keep my eyes closed without it."

"Humph!" commented a subaltern. He made a grimace as though he had tasted something unpleasant.

"What is it?" asked the next man. "Did you see a ghost?"

"Yes; an enlisted man we shot in Burmah. He did the same thing. It reminded me of it."

"She *does* take it rather seriously," whispered the other.

The blackboard hung like a curtain at one end of the room. There was no light near it, and it formed a black background against which Helen Page's figure and head stood out distinctly. She was a very beautiful woman, with great masses of black hair, which she wore back from her forehead. Her face was lovely rather than classic, and typically American in its frank confidence of her own innocence and of others towards her, and in its cleverness. She wore a gown of black satin, covered with tiny glittering spangles, that fitted her figure closely, leaving her arms and shoulders bare. It was a most unusual gown, and strongly suggestive of things theatrical, like a Columbine in mourning, or the wicked fairy who rises through a trap in the pantomime. On another woman it would have been bold, but on her it only made the face above it appear more lovely and innocent by contrast. It was as incongruous as a girl's face in a suit of armor.

But the costume fitted the moment with peculiar appropriateness, and as the girl raised her bare arm to write, she looked like a blind prophetess or a beautiful witch, who might transform them all into four-footed animals. She appeared so well standing in outline against the background, with the lights playing over the spangles, that both the men and the women present were more intent upon her than upon what she was about to do. Bannerman congratulated himself on his good fortune. He was enough of a showman to feel the effect she had produced, and, like a clever stage-manager, left to her the centre of the stage, while he kept his own person in the background of the picture.

"Are you ready?" he asked.

The girl's left arm hung straight at her side, with the palm turned out, so that the tips of her fingers touched those of the mind-reader as he stood with bowed head behind her. Miss Page moved her right hand slightly in assent.

And then, as though some subtle contact had been established between them by which the two individual minds moved in common, her right arm raised itself, and she began to grope across the board with a piece of chalk as though to find the starting-point. Her hand stopped high above her head, and the chalk scratched on the board and left behind it a queer jumble of Arabic figures. The arm rested in mid-air, and the girl's face, with her eyes still closed, bowed itself, as though she were listening and waiting for further instruction.

Bannerman glanced past her to the writing on the board. He turned his face to the audience, without losing his hold on the girl's finger-tips, and translated aloud, "His Excellency—" There were many present entitled to that prefix, and several who had already recognized it as it was written out before them. There was no question but that the sentence, so far, was in the most correct Arabic.

"He has established what he claims to do already," whispered Hoffmeyer Bey to Bannerman's ward. The girl nodded her head. Her lips were parted, and she was breathing quickly.

The chalk moved again, hesitated, and stopped. The mind-reader read over to himself what was written. There was a strange look on his face which told nothing, but there was something deprecatory in his tone as he said aloud, "His Excellency, the British Minister—"

There was a movement in the surrounding circle as though they had each felt that the affair had taken on a more intimate and personal complexion. And though each assured himself that what was to follow was but a compliment from the English showman to the English lord, there was something so uneasy in the manner of the mind-reader that the fancy of each took alarm, and the interest of all became deeply engaged.

7

The girl still stood trancelike and with bowed head, while her arm moved across the black surface of the board, but in the bearing of the mind-reader there was the dismay of one who finds the matter in hand growing beyond his control, and with this there was the touch of fear. It was in a tone so low that it barely penetrated the length of the room that he read the broken phrase which followed—"visits the opera to-morrow night—" he said.

As he pronounced these words there was a sudden movement in the circle about him, coming from no one person, and yet so apparent in its significance that each looked furtively at his neighbor, and dropped his eyes, or turned them anxiously towards the blackboard. Bannerman raised his body, and straightened himself as though he was about to speak further, but the scratching and tapping of the chalk upon the board interrupted him, and he dropped his head. It was as though he did not wish to see the completion of his work.

The voice of the young American Minister from the back of the room broke the tense stillness of the moment. He gave a long indrawn sigh of appreciation. "Mene, Mene, Tekel, Upharsin," he quoted, mockingly.

"Silence!" Hoffmeyer Bey commanded, half rising from the divan. And the silence he commanded answered him. The air of the room seemed charged with electricity. It was as though every one present were part of a huge battery; but no one moved. The scratching on the board ceased. The girl's arm dropped to her side, and the chalk fell and broke upon the floor.

Bannerman raised his eyes and read the completed phrase in a voice in which fear and a certain exultation were strangely blended.

"His Excellency the British Minister," he translated, "visits the opera to-morrow night at the risk of his life."

His voice died away as though afraid of its own daring, and there was complete stillness.

Then Immen Pasha stepped quickly into the centre of the room. "Bring back those lights," he commanded. He strode hastily to where the mind-reader stood, picking up the scarf Miss Page had dropped upon the floor as he did so, and drawing it across the surface of the board.

Miss Page opened her eyes, and closed them again as though they were heavy with sleep. She shivered slightly like one awakening, and ran her left hand up and down her other arm. Immen Pasha's movements as he swept the board caused her to raise her head, and her interest seemed to awaken.

"Oh, how curious!" she said. "Did I write that?"

The sound of her voice seemed to set free a spell that had been put upon the room, and there was a sudden chorus of nervous laughter and of general exclamation, above which could be heard the voice

of the British Minister, saying : " No ; he was before my time ; but I remember Maskelyne and
Cook at their place in Piccadilly, and they were
most amusing. They used to—"

The boyish faces of the English subalterns had
grown masklike and expressionless. They unconsciously drew together in little groups of red,
and, discovering this, instantly parted again. The
diplomats were smiling and chattering volubly;
the native Egyptians alone maintained their pla-
cidity of manner. Immen Pasha pushed his way
hurriedly to the side of the English Minister's
wife.

"There is a supper," he said, bowing gravely.
"It has been awaiting us some time. Will you
allow me ?"

The English woman smiled distantly, and fluttered her fan. "It is so late," she said, "I am
afraid we shall have to ask you to let us go."

Through the open windows of the street below
could be heard the voices of the servants calling
for the British Minister's carriage, and it seemed to
be for all an alarming signal of departure. So
hastily did they make their adieux that it seemed
as though each one feared to be left among the
last.

Young Page overtook Prince Panine as the
latter was hurrying on towards the Khedival
Club. "Going my way, Panine?" he asked. "I
say," he went on, "what a shame it broke up so
soon ! Immen had a fine supper for us, and I *am*

hungry. Helen and that mind-reading chap spoiled the whole evening between them."

Panine turned his head and surveyed his young companion in the darkness. " Yes," he said, " between them they spoiled several things."

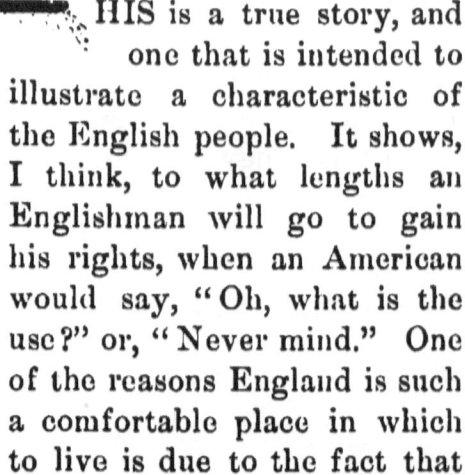

THIS is a true story, and one that is intended to illustrate a characteristic of the English people. It shows, I think, to what lengths an Englishman will go to gain his rights, when an American would say, "Oh, what is the use?" or, "Never mind." One of the reasons England is such a comfortable place in which to live is due to the fact that the English people have this peculiar habit of fighting for their rights, by letters to the *Times,* or by taking the numbers of cabmen and policemen and appearing against them in the morning, or by sending war-ships into strange harbors where the window-panes of some English merchants have been smashed. If there were elevated roads in London, the clerk who lives in Kensington would not hang and swing from a strap on his way to and from the city. He would see that he was given the seat for which he had paid. The American is too busy and too good·

natured to fight for his rights, so he continues to
stand from Rector Street to Harlem, and to walk
over unclean streets, and sees the beautiful green
park at the Battery taken from him and turned
into a railroad terminus. He will learn, in time,
that the reason the Englishman has better roads
and better streets and better protection for his life
and property is because he " makes a kick about
it," and protests and growls and is generally dis-
agreeable until he gets what he wants. Good-
nature is not always a virtue, and sometimes the
easy-going person is a very selfish one, too. Equally strong with his desire to have his rights is the
Englishman's deference for the rights of others.
He shows this deference by respecting the English law, which makes those rights good. There
was a young woman in England who told me that
she and seven or eight other young people had
tramped in single file through a gentleman's dining-room one evening, while he and his guests
were at dinner, in order to establish a right of
way. The Englishman had built his house on a
meadow directly across a pathway that had been
used for centuries, and once a year the young
people of the neighboring estates marched across
his lawn, and up his stairs, and through his house,
in order that he should remember that the right
of way still existed. She was an exceedingly shy
and well-bred young person, and of a family quite
as old as the right of way, but it apparently did
not strike her that she was rude in tramping

through a stranger's house, or, indeed, that she was doing anything but a public duty. And the interesting point of the story to me was that the English householder, instead of getting a Winchester and driving the young trespassers off of his lawn, should have had so full an appreciation of their right to question his right that he simply bit his lips and went to law about it.

There was an Irishman in the same county who lived in a small cottage on an estate, and who was in the habit of crossing from it to another through the gateway of a very distinguished and noble gentleman. He had done this for twenty years, and when the noble gentleman came into some more money and hung two fine iron gates between the posts, the Irish laborer took a crow-bar and broke the hinges on which they hung, and tramped over them on his way. He was put in jail for this for a month, at the end of which time he went after his crow-bar and tore the gates down again. When he had been in jail five times in six months, the people round about took up his case, and the right of way was declared a just one, and the gates came down forever. The Englishman will go further than this; he will not only fight for his rights, but he will fight for some other man's rights; he will go out of his road to tramp through a gentleman's property simply because the people in the neighborhood are disputing for right of way with him. I heard of three young barristers when I was in London who went on a walking-tour, and who laid out their route entirely with the purpose in view of taking in all the disputed rights of way in the counties through which they passed, and who cheerfully sacrificed themselves for the good of others by forcing their way into houses and across private grounds and by tearing down hedges.

This brings me to the particular right-of-way case in which I was involved, and of which I was appointed chronicler. I have been somewhat tardy in bringing the true story of this inglorious Oxford movement to the attention of the world; but now that it is to be written it will be given fully and with all possible detail, as befits so important an event in the history of the struggles for English liberty.

The Balliol Eight had bumped the boat in front that day, and were celebrating the fact with a dinner. I remember this dinner very well, because each of the eight had come to me in a friendly way during the afternoon, and had told me not to dress for dinner, as only bounders and cads wore dress clothes at a "wine." I accordingly came in flannels, and found the entire eight in the proper garments of evening, and with a pained and surprised look at my appearance, and when I demanded with some indignation why they had put me in such a position, they all denied ever having spoken to me at any time on the subject of dress, and apologized for my appearance to the other guests by explaining that I came from America, where evening dress was unknown. The guests accepted this as an interesting fact, and the eight grinned together in unison at the success of what they considered a very subtle practical joke. But I had my revenge, as they were still in training for Henley, and could eat nothing but cold meat, and so were forced to look on at the celebration of their victory by the only men present who had in no possible way contributed towards it. It was near the close of the dinner when the Hon. Hubert Howard, who pulled bow that day, rapped for silence, and when he had obtained it, announced gravely that he was looking for volunteers to join him in an expedition which promised much excitement, possible danger, and the ultimate success of which would bring liberty to many British subjects. Having gained the centre of the stage by this declaration, he stood up and further explained himself. He began with the deliberation of one who has a long story before him, and who means to tell it with all possible detail.

"Last summer," he began, "a chap named Curzon started to row from Stratford to Warwick with Harry Farmer, the gentleman on my right, whose work at stroke, I may add parenthetically, so largely contributed to our success of this afternoon." Mr. Farmer blushed at this and bowed his head, and everybody except the boy who wanted Farmer's place in the boat rapped with his knife-

handle and cried "Hear! hear!" in patronizing
tones.

"They rowed about seven miles," Howard continued, "until they were stopped by a barrier of
chains and iron rods across the river at Charlecote. The Charlecote estate, as you know, belongs to the Lucy family, and their land runs on
both banks of the Avon. They keep deer there,
and they claim that the excursionists from Warwick and Stratford, who row up and down the
river, frighten these deer. As you may remember,
the Lucys were always very particular about their
deer; they, or one of them, had Shakespeare himself up for killing a deer, and so handed themselves down to an inglorious immortality. Well,
they've put this iron barrier up now to keep the
boats out, and they've marked the river that
runs through their lands ' Private Water.' When
Farmer and Curzon discovered it, they rowed back
to a village and borrowed some tools and broke
the barrier down, and rowed on into the private
water, for which the agent of the estate took
Farmer's name, and told him he would summon
him to the high courts for trespass and destruction of private property. That was just a year
ago this June, and they haven't summoned him
yet, and they never will. And why? Why, because they are afraid, because they know they've
no more right to block that thoroughfare than
they have to build a wall across the Strand. Suppose a man owned a house on both sides of the

Strand, that wouldn't give him the right to run
a fence between his two properties, would it? Of
course it wouldn't.   Well, that's what these people have done.   Now we have been correspond-
ing with the Stratford Rowing Club, and they
tell us that the barrier has been built up again,
and they want to know if we won't go there and
break it down.   They're afraid to do it themselves, you see, because they live too near to
Charlecote, and the Lucys might make it unpleasant for them.   So Farmer and I are going down
there to-morrow or next day to tear down that
barrier, and any other gentleman who wants to
sacrifice himself for the sake of liberty can come
with us.   I call for volunteers."

There was much confusion and questioning and
mocking laughter.

"Right on our side?" demanded Howard.
"There never was a case with so much right
on one side.   It is overbalanced with right.   And
we've documents and pictures and things, and
we're going to nail the documents to a church
door.   There's a precedent for that; and I speak
to address the populace.   Mr. —— here," pointing to the father of one of the crew, "is an attorney, and though he won't let his son go with us,
he'll be our legal adviser, and Davis will be
chronicler and treasurer.   Davis, you Americans
are always talking about your love of liberty, and
here's a chance to exhibit it.   Besides, somebody
must be treasurer, or we can't go."

EXHIBIT " A " —CHARLECOTE HOUSE WITHOUT THE BARRIER—From an old Engraving

I temporized by saying that I should like to
hear from the legal adviser now instead of later,
when his advice would not perhaps be so valu-
able. The legal adviser smiled, and asked what
these documents of Howard's might be.

"One of them is an order in Privy Council,
issued by Charles II., declaring that the Avon
must be kept clear and open from Coventry to
the Severn; and we've got an old engraving of
Charlecote which proves conclusively that there
was no barrier there as late as 1790 ; and we also
have indirect backing in the fact that the Earl of
Warwick had to get an act of Parliament passed
before he could put up a barrier at Warwick
Castle, which is a step the Lucys have never
taken."

The legal adviser, after a pause, asked if Howard rested his case there, and on the Honorable
Hubert's replying that he did, the legal adviser
instantly withdrew from it. "I don't believe
you really want an attorney," he said, "though
you'll need one badly enough before you get
through."

But they were not at all frightened, and to the
American there was something particularly amusing in the idea of destroying a gentleman's private property on the strength of a document issued three hundred years back in the past. I
wanted to see what an English householder would
do under the circumstances ; I could guess how
the American householder would act. So it was

agreed that I should supply the money to bail
them out in case of their being arrested, if they
would supply the copies of the order in council
and the weapons for the attack. I was also to act
as photographer and chronicler of the expedition,
and to help enroll two other men. Further than
this I refused to strike a blow for the cause of
British liberty; but as it turned out we all had to
strike several blows.

We went down to Stratford third class, with
three sledge-hammers and three crow-bars in a
green-baize cricket-bag, at which the guards
would make a grab, and then drop it with a crash
upon the platform, with the final conviction, as we
drew out of the station, that they had fallen upon
a kit of burglar's tools. There were five in the
party—Howard and Farmer, T. P. Rogers, the
Captain of the Eight, and Murray, all of Balliol
College, and myself. There was another man
coming, who had been asked chiefly on account of
his name, but he overslept himself, and so missed
all the glory. Howard tried to get several other
titles for the same reason, as he thought he would
impress the police; but their owners strangely
enough objected, and for the same reason, saying
that the police were about the last people they
had any desire to impress. We told them they
had no sporting blood, and when they read this
they will be sorry they did not take the chance
we gave them to add further lustre to their an-
cient and distinguished names. We called our-

selves the Sons of Liberty, and when we arrived
at Stratford distributed our orders in council from
the top of the coach, and left them at the doors of
several houses belonging to gentlemen connected
with the local government and the Stratford Rowing Club. There was no church on our way to
the river, so Howard could not nail one of the
orders to its door, and we were in too much of
a hurry to wait for him while he addressed the
populace.

"Little they know," Howard said, as he pulled
away in the boat we had hired at the landing,
"as they go idly by, that we are going to
strike a blow for their rights and liberties. To
them we are merely a party of rowing-men out
for a lark, and that bag which is filled with
destruction contains nothing more terrible than
luncheon."

We all wished that it did contain nothing
more terrible than luncheon before we had
rowed very far, for the Avon seemed to run
uphill, and at places we all had to get overboard
to lighten the boat, and to pull her over the
shoals, while we stood knee-deep in the water.
By two o'clock we had covered five of the seven
miles before us, and had eaten and rested at a
little village where the innkeeper was very rude
to us.

"There again," said Howard, "you see the
ingratitude which makes martyrs. The innkeeper doesn't know that we are going to in-

crease his Sunday trade for travellers at least
two pounds a week. He thinks we are a lot of
vagabonds, and now that I come to look at the
rest of you, I don't much blame him. But it is
always thus with great reformers. They suffer
that others may reap the benefit. To obtain liberty—"

"Oh, look where you are steering us to!" cried
Rogers, "and don't talk so much."

"You're getting rattled, T. P.," Howard called
back cheerfully. "It's not too late to drop out if
you choose."

We were all rather silent. The rich green
banks lay level on either side of us, uninhabited
save for an occasional fisherman dozing beneath
a bunch of willows and for the birds that sang to
us across the meadows. And only half a mile
ahead we saw a row of great trees and an old
water-mill, which, so Farmer explained to us in a
whisper as though he was afraid the birds might
overhear him, marked our near approach to the
Charlecote lands.

"It's only another bend of the river now, and
then you can see the barrier yourselves. There
will be no one about," he added, with great indifference—"at least, I think not. The barrier is
over a quarter of a mile from the house, and the
family seldom walk there. We can hack it down
and get away again," he added, reassuringly, "before they know what is going on."

We all looked more cheerful.

"'THERE, NOW, DON'T YOU TAKE ON SO'"

"Let's go on to Warwick and break down that
barrier, too," cried Howard. "We might as well
make a clean sweep of the river while we're out.
What do you think?"

None of us said what we thought.. We were
rather quiet, all save Howard, whose delight and
excitement were rising visibly.

"Now look again, Farmer," he cried, as the
boat swung around the bend; "can you see it
from here?" Farmer, who was sitting in the
bow, stood up, and the Sons of Liberty rested on
their oars and waited. "Yes," he cried, excitedly,
"I can see it; we are almost on it. They've built
it up again, and then—oh, I say—" His voice
changed and died out so suddenly that we all
scrambled to our feet to see for ourselves without
waiting for an explanation.

What we saw, two hundred yards ahead of us,
was a barrier of iron rods and chains swung between heavy wooden posts that rose three feet
above the water-line, and the level turf stretching
away from one bank to a thick woods, and from
the other to a great mansion. But the turf between the barrier and the house was covered with
tents and marquees, and overrun with workmen
who were digging and hammering and filling the
place with life and movement. Instead of finding our barrier at a deserted bend of the river,
hidden by overhanging bushes, we had come upon
it apparently in the only populated spot upon the
Avon, and we stood silent and dumfounded like

8

criminals caught in a trap. It was Howard who
was the first to speak.

"I say," he exclaimed, delightedly, "we are going to have an audience, aren't we? I must say,
Farmer, it was rather civil of you to send them
word."

"They're making ready for an agricultural fair,
or a lawn-party, or something," growled Farmer.
"How could I know that? What shall we do
now?"

"Do?" said Murray. "What do you suppose?
We haven't travelled four hours in a third-class
compartment, and rowed seven miles uphill, to
go back again, have we?"

"Now, then," cried Howard, clutching the tiller-
ropes around him. "Pull up to it in style. Live-
ly, now. Bump her right into it." They fell
back in their places and shot at a racing pace
over the last stretch that lay between them and
the private water; when they came to the barrier they slowed up, and, unshipping their oars,
ran the boat up broadside against it. "Make
her fast there at both ends," Howard commanded,
standing up and laughing with excitement. "You
mustn't land. If you did, they would have us up
for trespass. We must attack it from the boat."

"Wait a minute," I shouted back; "I want
those orders in council put up first."

"Quite right," answered Howard. "Farmer,
run along the barrier and put one up on that tree
where they can see it."

"'YOU CAN'T GO THROUGH THERE, SIR!'"

March 9, 163⅚.

ORDER OF THE KING IN COUNCIL.

Sec : Windebank this day acquainted his Majesty, sitting in Council, that Wm. Sandys, of Fladbury, co. Worcester, had undertaken at his own cost to make the river Avon passable from Severn, where that river falls in near Tewkesbury, through counties Worcester, Gloucester, and Warwick, unto or near Coventry, and that he has been already at great charge therein ; also that Mr. Sandys intends to make passable a good part of the river Teme lying towards Ludlow, whereby the said counties may be better supplied with wood, iron, and pit coals which they want. It was ordered that commissions should be issued to persons of quality in each of the said counties, authorizing them to see that all persons interested in any lands, soil, mill, or other thing adjoining the rivers aforesaid be reasonably compounded with, and to call before them such persons as shall not be content to accept reasonable recompence for their estates whereof use is necessarily to be made. In such case the Commissioners are to assess such recompence to be given by Sandys as shall be just ; and if in a business so well approved by his Majesty the Commissioners find any persons factious or opposing, they are to certify their names to the board that such further order may be taken as shall be just. Lastly the Attorney General is to give his special furtherance in this undertaking.

See CALENDAR OF STATE PAPERS.
Edited by Bruce.
Longmans, 1866.

S—on—A CORPORATION RECORDS. AVON NAVIGATION.

Council Book C. p. 126.—
At a Hall held 9 January 1635.— " At this Hall a Writinge passed under o^r Comon Seale unto Wm Sandis esq. testifying b^r approbation comendacon and alowance of the makinge of the River of Avon passible for bringinge of Wares from sondrye places to this boroughe of Stratford."

do p. 200. Hall held 1 Oct. 1641.—"M^r. W^m. Sandes is to have the Comon Seale to a peticon to be Drawne by Mr Dighton for assistance in his navigacon and for mendinge the highewaies."

Farmer stepped over the side and on to the barrier, and worked his way along it as a sailor runs out on the bowsprit. When he had reached the bank farthest from the house and from the workmen, he nailed the order in council upon a tree which stood so close to the water's edge that it was used as a support for the barrier. It had all been done in a second of time, but one of the workmen on the estate had seen us coming and had run down to the edge of the bank to meet us.

"You can't go through there, sir," he called, waving with his hand. "That's private water, sir."

T. P. Rogers was on his knees working at the straps of the cricket-bag; he pulled out the sledge-hammers and held them up, and Howard swung one blindly and struck the lock of the gate that formed the centre of the barrier. The lock rattled, but the gate stood like a stone wall.

"First blood for us," Howard claimed. "Now, all together !"

The workman dropped his shovel and started on a run towards the house, calling to his mates. Some of them followed him, and others ran down to the water's edge and consulted together in great uncertainty. They were the first persons to show me that day that an Englishman knows when it is not his place to interfere, and that all things, even the resisting of an assault, must be done decently and with due regard for law and order. All of the Sons of Liberty had crow-bars or hammers in their hands now, and were striking frantically but impotently at the swinging chains. But as they were doing no possible damage, I advised them to stop until they could pick out the vulnerable point of the barrier, and while they were doing this I photographed them. The picture shows them when this photograph was being taken.

Each of us had an entirely different idea as to how the barrier should be attacked, and we were all shouting at once, and telling each other to "Hit it there, where it joins," or "Here, give it to me," or "I'll show you, let me have it," and "It is no use prying at that, knock it off with the sledge."

It was most exciting, and as the crow-bars struck the iron chains and the sledges rang on the gateway, the sparks flew brilliantly, so that one might have thought they were fighting their way out of prison instead of into a stretch of pretty water. They had changed the soft summer quiet of the Avon into the noisy clangor of a blacksmith-shop.

"How long did it take you to get this thing down last time, Farmer?" Howard gasped between strokes.

"An hour," said Farmer, who had lost his crowbar overboard, and was holding on to a post to steady the boat.

"An hour!" gasped Howard. "And we have to do it in five minutes." The Sons of Liberty

were not used to sledges or crow-bars, and the
boat rocked so violently as they swung their bod-
ies for each stroke that the water poured over the
sides, and one crow-bar after another was jerked
out of their hands and shot with a splash to the
bottom of the river. The bank was crowded now
with workmen and the servants of the Lucy household. A grave young man, who looked as though
he might be the agent of the estate, was the first
to arrive. He bit his nails and grinned feebly,
and then frowned sternly in much indecision. He
was followed closely by half a dozen stable-boys
in gaiters, and the butler and underservants struggling into their coats as they ran. They all
prowled up and down the bank like animals in
a cage, not two oars' length from us, or gathered in groups and whispered and laughed nervously. At every second stroke of the flying hammers they turned their heads to look back at the
house.

"You fellows had better hurry," I said. "Somebody's coming soon who means to do something.
They're waiting for him."

There was only one small hammer and a mean
little crow-bar left to us now, and the four colle-
gians stopped for lack of weapons and gazed hopelessly at the barrier, panting and covered with
muddy water and perspiration.

As each hammer or crow-bar had disappeared
I had called to the boys to jump in after it; but
they, in spite of the fact that they were already

wet and in dirty cricket flannels that would not have been hurt by a bath, had looked at me scornfully and made no answer. Now that the attack had stopped altogether, I besought them again. But Rogers only growled and asked if I wanted to drown him.

"I thought anybody could swim under water," I explained.

"Can you?" Rogers demanded.

"Why, yes," I answered, injudiciously.

"Then pull your clothes off and get over there, quick," cried Murray, who was the largest of them, "or we will throw you over. Jump now!"

There was at this time about forty people on the bank, and among them a dozen house-maids in white caps, chaperoned by a fat cook who was fanning herself, after her run, with a large checkered apron. I was going that evening to a country-house where I knew no one as yet, and was not, in consequence, dressed in shrunken cricket flannels. So for these two reasons I hesitated.

"Come, jump," said Howard; "you've got to help too."

Whenever a crow-bar had been carried away the crowd on the bank had cheered and jumped up and down with satisfaction, but when I got up and began to pull off my clothes there was an interested silence, and a hasty stampede on the part of the women, whose modesty and desire to see the outcome of the attack on the barrier pulled them both ways. It was very cold in the Avon, and the barrier had caught innumerable branches of trees on their way down-stream and had dropped them to the bottom, where they felt to the touch exactly like water-snakes, and suggested man-traps, though why any one should put a man-trap eight feet under water I cannot now imagine, but while I was crawling around feeling for sledge-hammers it seemed the most natural and probable thing for a person to do. I got all of the weapons but one, and as each showed above the water the boys yelled, and the crowd cheered too, as it promised more entertainment for them. Then they hauled me over the side and went at the gate again more carefully, so carefully, indeed, that once, when Murray lost his balance, he, sooner than let the hammer go, let himself go, and the result was that the force of the blow and the hammer's weight pulled him forward, and he hung himself up over the barrier as a horse does over a fence, with the important difference that all of the upper part of Murray's long body was under water while his legs were kicking wildly in the air. We pulled him back again, sputtering and coughing and with green moss and twigs and leaves sticking in his ears and hair, so that he looked like a water-nymph. We were all fighting the gate now, for they had given me a hammer that I might get warm again, and the lock was nearly gone; then two chains fell to the bottom, and the lock broke and the gate swung back, and with a triumphant yell we pulled and

pushed our boat head-forward into the private
water. We were not a moment too soon, for
across the lawn came a galloping cob swinging a
dog-cart behind him with three men clinging to
its top, and going at such a pace that the cart
rocked like a skiff at sea. They were the three
largest men I had ever seen. They were dressed
in keepers' knickerbockers and velveteen, and of
course I, being an American, expected they would
begin to shoot as they reached the bank. I supposed from what I had read of game-keepers in
Kingsley's novels that they would probably carry
shot-guns with sawed-off barrels, such as poachers
affect, and while carefully steering the boat into
the private water I was wondering how far a shot-
gun would carry, and whether sawing off the barrels would not make the shot scatter over a very
large surface. Howard, being an Englishman,
knew perfectly well that no one would shoot us,
so he hailed their approach gayly.

"Now it's getting exciting," he said. "Shall
we stop here and fight 'em, or go on to Warwick
and break down the other barrier?"

We admired his spirit very much, but we pointed out that we had established our point by destroying the barricade and entering the private
water, and that it was now a case for lawyers to
settle. So, in spite of Howard's remonstrances,
the boys pulled the boat's head around towards
Stratford. The keepers sprang from the cart
into a punt, and six of the grooms and servants

tumbled in after them, and with a single oar shoved after us in pursuit.

"Let's stop and board them," said Howard, who was sitting impotently in the bow. But Farmer said to go on, but not to hurry, or they would think we were running away. "Keep the stroke you have got, and talk about the weather," he said. But our dignified and leisurely departure went for nothing, for the first thing the keepers went for was the order in council. They were evidently not going to attack any one until they had read and digested this brief, and they judged that the piece of paper fluttering on the tree was ours. It served us as the child thrown to the wolves served the men in the sleigh, for by the time the keepers had puzzled it out, and what possible bearing it had on our destruction of their barrier, we had lighted our pipes and drifted gracefully out of sight around the bend.

"Such a lot of muffs I never did see," said Howard, who was in full mutiny. "Why didn't you row up alongside and bang them with the oars?"

"What's the good?" said Murray. "The barrier's down, isn't it? There were forty of them, and they'd have thrown us in a horse-pond, most likely; and that's not dignified. What's the use of rowing with keepers? 'Tisn't their barrier."

"Use?" said Howard. "Well, we'd have been arrested for one thing, and I could have made a speech too,"

"MURRAY CLUNG TO THE SLEDGE-HAMMER"

We lay on our oars and let the boat run with the rapid current, which was now with us, and we felt like patriots and heroes as the people in the occasional villages hurried to the banks to ask if the barrier was down, and on hearing that it was, started off with a shout to tell their neighbors. Then the boats of the Stratford Rowing Club began to appear, and the occupants asked the same question, and said, "That's good," and laughed at our muddy garments and dripping hair.

"We'll have a grand reception when we get to Stratford," said Howard, gleefully. "It will be all over the town by that time. Those orders of council we threw out will have stirred up their curiosity."

There was a nice old gentleman fishing from a punt about a mile from Stratford, and he regarded our dishevelled and disreputable appearance as we drifted towards him. "Are you the gentlemen," he inquired, doubtfully, "who went up to Charlecote to destroy the barrier?"

We said that we were. He regarded his bobbing float with interest, and then called after us, without raising his head:

"'They're waiting to give you a reception at the bridge. They will be glad to see you."

"Do you hear that?" asked Howard, triumphantly.

There was something about the nice old gentleman's manner that I did not fancy, and I said I thought we had much better tie the boat up to a

tree and make a run across country until we struck
a railroad station. "We can telegraph the man
where his boat is," I said, "and send the money
by mail. I don't want a reception."

But Howard would not hear of it. "Why, that's
the best part; that's our reward," he remonstrated.

"He wants to address the populace," said Farmer. "Let him alone." The bridge was black
with people, and many more were grouped along
the wharf and far up the bank.

"There must be a boat-race on," I suggested,
"and they're waiting for the finish."

"They're waiting for us!" shouted Howard, as
we turned the last bend. "Isn't it glorious?" he
chuckled.

But Farmer, who was pulling bow and looking
over his shoulder, suddenly threw himself forward on his oar. "Stop—back her!" he shouted.
"Look at the police!"

The entire constabulary force of Stratford was
gathered in brave array at the edge of the water,
with an inspector at their head, and our friends
the game-keepers and the nervous agent drawn
up beside them. A cob, smothered with lather
and with heaving sides, was standing on the bridge
hitched to a dog-cart, and told the story.

"They've beaten us," said Howard. "If we
had rowed instead of drifting, we should have
won easily."

We paddled up to the wharf, and the crowd on
the bridge cheered. Howard stood up and took

off his cap to the inspector. "Are you going to arrest us, Mr. Policeman?" he asked.

"We are," said that dignitary.

"Then we must ask you to stand just as you are for a minute until we photograph you. I have never been arrested, and I must have the pictures of the men who do it as souvenirs. Move up close," he said to us over his shoulder, "so that Davis can get a good focus; but don't get too close," he added, hastily, "or they'll grab us with a boat-hook."

We snapped the shutter at them several times from a safe distance, much to their disgust, but to the delight of the crowd, in whose eyes we were martyrs. The attitude of the inspector was strongly suggestive of an old hen on a bank worrying over young ducklings in the water.

"Are you coming out to us, sir," said Howard, "or do we have to come in to you?"

"Come, now, no nonsense," said the inspector; "we've been here long enough." So we ran the boat to the bank and gave ourselves up. The inspector and the agent whispered together and the game-keeper pointed at each of us.

"All of them?" said the inspector.

"All of them," repeated the agent.

My hopes of reaching the country-house at which I was promised began to grow infinitesimally small, and I fingered nervously at the bail-money in my pocket. "You are not a Stratford man?" said the inspector to Howard.

Howard replied in a very loud tone that he was not, but that that made no difference, as the liberties and rights of the people of Stratford were as dear to him as though he had always lived among them. The men in the back of the crowd said "'ear! 'ear!" at this, and some boys on the bridge who were too far off to know what was going on, leaned over the railing and shouted " Hoorar." The inspector frowned angrily and took out an imposing-looking blank book.

" Where do you live?" he asked, " if you live anywhere, and what's your name?" Howard gave his name, and Balliol College, Oxford, as his address. The reporters, who were looking over the inspector's shoulder as he wrote, whispered to him eagerly at this, and he stared at Howard's muddy garments and disreputable appearance and shook his head.

"This gentleman says that you're the son of Such a Person. Is that so?" he asked.

" Well, what if it is?" said Howard. " I say," he went on, eagerly turning to us, " this is my chance, isn't it; now I *will* address the populace." There was a broad row-boat turned bottom up, and Howard sprang on that and waved his hat at the crowd. "Gentlemen," he said, " the inspector has shown surprise that we should come all the way from Oxford to break down a barrier. We would go twice as far for as good a purpose. This gentleman without any shoes on has come all the way from America to do it, and we are

WE ARRIVED AT THE BRIDGE

glad and proud of what we have done. We are going to fight this case from court to court until it reaches the House of Lords, and then," he said, suddenly running up to the keeper and patting him on his broad chest, to which Howard's hand could just reach, "this keeper and I will walk up hand in hand to the bar of the House together and settle this thing between us."

The crowd cheered, and we applauded, and everybody laughed except the keeper, who was so overcome with the idea of walking hand in hand with a peer's son to the very bar of the House of Lords that he could only grin helplessly and rub one knickerbockered leg against the other. Then the inspector took the other names, and as T. P. was Captain of the Eight and a very famous man indeed, and as each man save myself gave Balliol College, Oxford, as his address, the crowd continued to laugh and cheer, and the inspector to look worried and confused.

"It certainly is a queer lark for gentlemen like you," he remonstrated, resentfully, "to come all that way just to break the peace — and dressed like that, too!" he added, as if that were criminal enough in itself.

The agent seemed to regret having mustered such a show of force, and assured us with infinite politeness that our names and not our persons would be quite sufficient for his purpose. So he and the keepers drove off in the cart, and the towns-people took us to the Red Lion, where they

gave us things to drink and made us fine speech-
es, and organized committees to take up subscrip-
tions and to fight our case.

That ends this famous story, which tells how
William Shakespeare was avenged, and the liberties of the Stratford Boating Club recognized.
But I grieve to relate that after I left England
Farmer was summoned to appear before the High
Court, where our order in council and our engraving of the Charlecote estate *without* the barrier
made no impression whatsoever, strange as it may
appear, upon the judges, who smiled our attorney
out of court, and made us pay eighty pounds for
sacrificing ourselves upon the altar of liberty. And
this in spite of the assurances from all parts of the
country which we had received by telegraph and
through the papers that we had done well.

But the cruelest cut of all, perhaps, is that in
Oxford, where this great movement of reform
originated, there are some who say that it was
not for the sacred cause of liberty that we broke
down the barrier, but in a trivial spirit of mischief. And thus are the motives of all great reformers misunderstood.

THE Ingrams were on their way home, and were only waiting in London until it was time to take the steamer from Southampton. Alice Ingram had seen Thorold's name on one of the bills that advertised the two-hundredth night of his new opera, and on the chance sent a note to the theatre, asking him to call at the Albemarle the next afternoon. She had not seen him since early in the spring, in Paris, when he had seemed in a fair way of being spoiled, and the reports kind friends had given her of him since were not encouraging.

Thorold was one of the Thorolds of Salem. All of his immediate ancestors had been born in Salem, and had gone back there to be buried, but had lived in Boston and on the Continent. The family had no particular characteristics, except the invariable good looks of its members and their strong Puritanism, which they had inherited, and which had developed itself in the case of the women into something very like prudery, and which had made prigs of the men. Their discreet actions and well-regulated lives had always shown as strong a family likeness as had their fine profiles, and when "Archie" Thorold developed into

9

a musical genius he was looked upon with suspicion as the only member of the family whose conduct before the world needed the slightest explanation.

He developed this taste very early in his life,
and composed Christmas anthems and hymn tunes
at the age of fifteen, at which time he was playing the organ in the Episcopal church at Salem.
Later, while at Harvard, he wrote the music for
the Hasty Pudding theatricals; and two of the
comic songs of that production, notably "The
Night that McManus went Broke," were sung all
over the United States.   Thorold's elder brothers
did not regard this as fame, and hoped he would
give up writing music of any class after leaving
college; but he went off to Baireuth, and from
there to Munich, from which place they heard of
him occasionally as being very busy studying
thorough-bass.   He returned each winter, and
went to dances with his sisters in a perfectly ra-
tional and charming way; but he was off again
in the spring, and when next they heard of him
Lady Maud Anstey's amateurs and some officers
had played and sung in a cantata he had written
them for a charity entertainment; and a romantic
opera, called "The Crusaders," of which he had
written both score and book, was about to be
produced in Paris.   This met with success in
London, and later in New York as well, and his
family finally, on the first night of the opera's
production in Boston, experienced the sensation

of seeing one of their number leading an orchestra. It was a marked social as well as theatrical event, and Thorold looked very young and
very much in earnest as he leaned forward and
beat his bâton at the violins and scowled at the
ladies of the chorus. It was after this that he
wrote "The Well of Truth."

This was a love-song, and almost any one with
the most indifferent voice could make others with
any feeling weep or sigh as it was sung to them.
When Thorold sang it himself at the Tavern
Club or in the drawing-rooms, without any rolling of the eyes or any show of interest save a
deep scrutiny of the keys, every woman in the
room felt he was singing it at her, and every man
present thought that if he had that voice and a
face like that he could win love honestly from
any one. Young women sang "The Well of
Truth" to pianos and parlor organs all over the
country, and older people requested it for encores,
as it seemed to bring back to them something of
their youth; and even when it had been scattered abroad by street organs and rearranged to
waltz time it lost nothing of its popularity, but
seemed to gain in favor as it grew older and
more familiar.

By the time Thorold's second opera had been
produced people had grown tired of saying what
a wonder it was his head was not turned, and
wanted something new to say, so they said it was
such a pity so nice a boy allowed himself to be

spoiled, and the critics and paragraphers who had
stumbled over one another in their haste to be
among the first to recognize the new composer
now hastened to point out that the young genius
who had awakened to find himself famous had
never quite recovered from the shock.   Thorold
had not given much weight to the papers at the
first, and so did not mind their change of tone at
the last, or their hints that he was repeating himself, and that he was, after all, only a clever
plagiarist, and had too retentive a memory.   This
had been said of better men than he.   But he did
mind what his friends said, for he believed that
they could be actuated only by interest in his
best self, and he was at that time engaged in
watching his best self critically to see how well
it was withstanding this sudden shock of admiration and easily given sympathy.   He had a not
very original theory, for which his Puritan ancestors were responsible, that the quality of his
work depended on the quality of his own life,
and that as he cheapened himself and took life
less seriously, so his work would become less pure
and strong, and would show to all the world his
each easy step from grace.   No one gave him
credit for such theories ; he, naturally, did not
exploit them, and he had set his rules of life so
much higher than his neighbors had found it con-
venient to place theirs that they could not follow
him.   Had he married and become the master of
one household, as his brothers had done, he would

have found his principles much more easy to
carry out than he did in the atmosphere and society into which his work and his sudden celeb-
rity led him. But his friends did not consider
this either.

"Confound my Puritan ancestors, anyway!"
he said one day to Alice Ingram. "It's all their
doing. They gave me an artistic temperament
and an iron-bound conscience, and expect me to
decide which one of them is going to win. They
won't compromise, of course."

"That's right," said Miss Ingram, relentlessly.
"Put all the blame on your ancestors. Of course
you have no responsibilities."

"Alice," Thorold protested, meekly, "don't you
think a Good Angel might occasionally be sym-
pathetic?"

"You know I don't like being called a Good
Angel," Miss Ingram answered. "It sounds like
such a horrid sort of a person; and, besides, you
get sympathy enough from silly girls, and a lot
of married women who ought to know better."

This was in Paris. Since then the world, as
far as the world could judge, went very well with
Archibald Thorold; but Miss Ingram, through
mutual friends and from his infrequent letters,
knew that a struggle was going on between the
artistic temperament and the Puritan conscience,
and she was very sad as to the result. It seemed
to her that the very fact that the world was so
ready to excuse so much in so charming and brill-

iant a young man for the work he had done made
it all the more necessary for him to keep himsel.
untarnished from the world, and to refuse to accept its indulgences, because they were so easily
given.

It was this quality in Alice Ingram that at-
tracted Thorold. She had appealed to him when
he had first met her, just as she had appealed to
many other men, through her cleverness and her
remarkable beauty; but what had fascinated him
the most, and what had kept him true to her in
thought, if not in deed, was her unrelenting quality—the fact that she never excused a weakness
in herself or in others, that she would have no
compromises, and that, as he protested, she would
" never let up on him " when he offered excuses.
Whether it was that in the past she had broken
somebody's heart, or half a dozen hearts, and was
repentant, or whether some one had broken her
heart and she was wise, he did not know or care.
It was not her past which interested him, and
his interest in her future was problematical. He
would not go to her unworthily, and yet life was
made so very easy for him as he was. He believed that it was this unrelenting quality which
made him regard her more seriously than he did
other women, and he thought that if she should ·
ever fail him in this, her great beauty and her
mind would count for nothing, and she would become to him like any other of the half-dozen
women he knew best.

He was standing as she entered the room, looking out of the window, and she noticed how tired he looked and dissatisfied and pale. Generally when he met her he came towards her quickly enough, and held her hand longer than was necessary, but to-day he simply turned and nodded and smiled oddly at her, as though he were rather more curious to see her than glad. So she walked over beside him, and they stood looking out at the carriages and hansoms on Piccadilly.

"It is very nice to see you again," she said. "It was just a chance—I saw your name in large red letters at Waterloo Station as we came in." He was regarding her intently, as though he were trying to recollect where he had seen her before. "I didn't know whether you could come or not," she went on. "You are in such demand now, they tell me."

"Of course you know very well," he said, with that directness which was one of his most satisfactory qualities, "that I would have come, whether I had had engagements or not. But I had meant not to come at first."

"Oh, you had meant not to at first!" she repeated. She sat down behind the tea things, and began moving them about. He seemed to her to be laboring under a mood or some excitement, and she thought it best to give him time to develop it.

"Yes," he said, slowly and distinctly, "I thought I would not come, because I did not want to introduce you to the kind of man you do not care to know."

"How tragic!" she said. "May I make you some tea?"

"I did not mean to be tragic," he went on, impassively. "It is quite true. I am not at all the man you used to know. No one can know that better than I. And I had so much liking for you —and for the man you used to know — that I thought it would be kinder to us both if I let you go home without seeing me again."

"But you did come."

"Yes, I came," he answered, after some moments' consideration, "because, I suppose, I still believe in miracles, and because I had a forlorn hope that if I could get a good strong tonic and my conscience could have an electric shock, it might begin to work again. It was just a chance. I hadn't much reason to believe it would."

She occupied herself for some little time with the cups in front of her, and said: "Of course it is very manly and brave in you to tell me this— to say, 'Here I am in a very bad way, and if you cannot help me no one can.' That makes it so pleasant for me. Of course you have no responsibility in the matter at all. It is something you cannot possibly mend. What a baby it is!"

"No," he said, doubtfully, as though he had been weighing her words and had found them wanting, "it is not the least use. It doesn't hurt me at all. It sounds like something I had learned

at school. I had hoped it would. I have gone so
far now, or I have gone so low, that I can quite
recognize the force of all the arguments on the
other side, and go the wrong way without a
pang." He looked up and smiled. "It is too
late. I am quite hopeless."

"You are quite changed," she said, dryly.

"Changed! Thank you." He laughed un-
pleasantly. "That is the mildest word any one
has used yet. But I've really no right to complain; the strongest things they say are quite
true."

"What! *all* they say?"

"Well, if the particular stories they have told
you are not true, others equally discreditable are.
It's the same thing."

She rested her chin on the knuckles of her
hand and studied him for some time. He looked
back at her without wavering and without interest.

"I think," she said, "he has been sitting up
very late at night, and has not had sleep enough;
he has been playing and working too hard, and he
has been taking himself too seriously. Of course,"
she added, with the air of one who wishes to be
quite fair, "there are some things a man must go
through with which we women go around."

"Thank you," Thorold said, grimly. "You are
very good, but I have excuses enough. I can supply *them* myself."

The girl showed no sign of annoyance at this,

but still regarded him thoughtfully. "The only saving clause I see," she said, "is your saying you hoped something might step in to help you. Of course, if a man wants to be saved from himself he has won half the fight, and he must win the other half, too. No young woman is going to do it."

"The pathetic part of it is," he answered, "that I don't want to be helped or to be saved. I said I did, but I don't, really. I like it better as it is. And it only makes it worse to pretend to be any better than I am, and to cheat myself and my friends into thinking I am. A man is no better than what he wishes to be at his worst moment. You cannot judge him by what he happens to want to be when he is worked up to do great things and inspired by other people. I *like* to waste my time and to have no responsibilities, and I like dangling in boudoirs better than working, and I like the cheap admiration of a lot of fools better than the esteem of a few friends; and I can't, for the life of me, see why I should live a lie to them and myself, and cover up the true badness that's in me. And I am not going to any longer. If I cared to be fine and strong, it would be natural enough and easy to be so; and if I don't care for that, it is only hypocrisy and waste of time to be anything that looks like it. I came here to-day to tell you this myself, so that there could be no longer any doubt in your mind, and I don't want you to waste any more thought or friendship on any one as unworthy of both as myself I felt I was deceiving you, and I wanted you to know. That's why I came. I never deceived you before, and I wished you to know—I want you to be disgusted with me and understand me just as I am. The man you knew is gone, and you—"

Miss Ingram stood up, and clasped her hands quickly in front of her. "What have I to do with it?" she said, coldly. "You are not answerable to me."

She crossed the room to the window, and then faced him again. "Listen to me, Archie," she said. "This may be a mood or a pose, or it may be that you are only run down and overworked and nervous, and are exaggerating these wickednesses you hint of." He was about to interrupt her, but she raised her hand for him to let her continue. "But you cannot afford to do it too often. It is not a pretty pose, and were I not a long-suffering lady, I would not tolerate it for a moment. It takes all the affection I have for you and all my patience not to accept you at your word, and tell my people you are not the sort of young man they should allow their daughter to see. But I think we know each other pretty well now, and I think there is more overwork and late hours in this than anything else. But you cannot keep it up too long. Bad habits are just as hard to overcome at the end as good habits, and even Balzac's twenty-five years of virtue which cannot be overcome in a day,

can be overcome in a year. And if you *will* live
in a bad atmosphere you cannot expect to be as
strong and healthy as you would be if you lived
in the open air. I don't think it is worse than
that. You have allowed yourself to stay in a bad
atmosphere which does not agree with you. Don't
be afraid to run away. I have a great regard for
the man who runs away. If you are wise, and the
boy I know, you will pack your things to-night
and sail with us to-morrow, and leave all these
women and worldly young men behind you. Come
and play with me on the steamer, and spend the
summer with all your old friends at the old places,
where no one thinks you're a great man, and where
you won't see your picture in all the shop windows. That's really what you need. What do
you say?" She stopped and looked at him, but he
made no response, and she hurried on, as though
to cover up the fact that she had failed to move
him. "I can't understand some women," she cried,
impatiently; "they fall in love with a man because he is good and strong, and then they at
once begin to pull down the very things they
most admire in him. And I cannot understand
your sex either. You are such, children. You
make such problems and difficulties out of nothing. Why, it is as simple as animal alphabets.
A is an ape, and B is a bear. That's all it is—
just animal pictures. There is no question of
which to choose, or there shouldn't be, for a man
like you. What is the admiration of a lot of silly

women to the friendship of such friends as you
have, who care for the best that is in you? How
can you tell me there is any question about it—or
of which to choose?"

Thorold stood up smiling, and shook his head.
"I tell you it is no use, Alice," he said. "I am
honestly not worth it. I've given up, and I'm
going my own way. All these things you say
have lost their meaning. They don't reach me.
It is like some one talking a language I have forgotten. You needn't think it didn't hurt at first
when I saw which way I was going, but it doesn't
hurt now. I like it, and do it because I like it,
and I am not going to pretend I don't. I am
pleasing myself entirely. Don't look at me like
that. I'm not worth troubling about. I'm not
worth a thought from you, Alice." He stopped,
and added, sharply, "Certainly not tears."

"I'm not ashamed of my tears, if there are any
in my eyes," the girl answered; "but," she added,
slowly, "I should think *you* would be."

"I'm not," he said, simply. "Think of it—I'm
not! That's what I've come to. And yet," he
added, with a sudden exclamation, "there was a
time when every word you spoke meant—"

"Stop! don't!" she said, breathlessly, and holding her hands before her, "don't! How could
you?"

Thorold took a step backward and bit his lip,
and so stood, with his face flushing, and with his
eyes bent towards the floor. Then he raised his

head and smiled grimly. "That, I should think," he said, "would convince you of the truth of all I have said. I can't go much lower than that, can I?" He did not look at her again, but turned and left the room without trying to take her hand or saying good-bye. When he reached the street he stepped into a hansom at the door and sank back on the cushions with a laugh. "That was my last chance," he murmured, grimly. "It has failed, and now I can go to the devil with a perfectly clear conscience." He raised the lid of the hansom with his stick. "To St. John's Wood," he said to the driver.

Miss Beatrice or "Trix" Gwynn, who lived next door to Mrs. Inness, out St. John's Wood way, posed for the great artists and all of the fashionable photographers. You saw her reproduced in many paintings at the different exhibitions as a very English-looking Greek maiden, with fluffy yellow hair and round baby-like eyes. She was very much of a fool. She lived in a little house shut off from the world by a big wall, and she was understood to enjoy an income from the sale of her photographs, on which income she kept a brougham. She had two very dear friends, the beautiful Mrs. Inness and Captain Cathcart, a very brave and good-natured but simple-souled gentleman and officer of the Inniskillen Dragoons.

"I can't stop, thanks," Thorold said. "I just came to see if you and Cathcart would come in to supper at my rooms to-night; and—I should be

very glad if you would bring your friend Mrs.
Inness with you ; that is, you know, if she will
not mind my not knowing her. Or I'll book you
a box at the piece to-night, if you like, and I'll
join you there. Perhaps that would be better,
and we can make the supper an after-thought.
Mrs. Inness might prefer it that way."

"Oh, Mildred won't mind," said Miss Gwynn,
lazily. "She'll come if I ask her ; and then, besides, she's just dotty to meet you. She told me,
when I said I'd met you, that she'd rather—"

"Well, that's all right, then," Thorold interrupted, hastily. "It's very good of you to come.
Tell Cathcart to ask for the box as he goes in."

There were several things Thorold had promised himself if he ever let everything go, and
now that he had determined to let everything go
he wanted to begin with them at once, and make
going back an impossibility. Mrs. Inness was
not one of the things he had promised himself,
but she would serve as well as another. He had
seen her often, and had heard of her, of course.
She was a very beautiful woman of large, graceful figure, who looked more like an Italian, in
spite of her yellow hair, than an English woman,
and she carried herself so well that she should
have been a duchess instead of what she was.
Her husband was, or had been, an officer in India,
where he had died, or where she had left him
still living : no one of her acquaintances was
particular enough to know or care which. She

sat at Thorold's right at supper, and smiled upon him encouragingly. She was very much pleased with everything, and assured him that his *chef* was as much of a master of his art as his master was of his.

"I and my cook thank you," said Thorold, gravely.

"Mildred always goes wrong when she tries to be grand," Miss Gwynn whispered to Cathcart. "I tell her to just sit still and let them look, and not talk."

Cathcart laughed good-naturedly, and asked Thorold's servant over his shoulder to pass the lobster.

"And now," Miss Beatrice went on, wickedly, "she's telling him her anecdotes of the aristocracy. That's the way she always begins with a new man. She lays siege to him. *I* don't bother with 'em, *I* don't."

Cathcart answered with a heavy bow and a whisper, which caused the young model to wave her fork at him playfully and say, "Oh, *you, you* don't count."

Mrs. Inness had tried several moves; openly expressed admiration for his work did not seem to answer. Either Thorold had had a surfeit of it or wanted it more highly spiced, for he did not seem to heed it. So she adopted a politely fashionable tone, and talked of the great people of the hour and of their escapades, until she suspected from a light in Thorold's eyes that he was already

intimately familiar with what had come to her at
second hand, and that he knew it had come to her
at second hand. So she became herself, and was
bold and amusing and daring and familiar. Thorold watched her without attempting to conceal
his admiration, not for her, but for her beauty,
which was unquestionable. It was of the impe-
rious stamp that invited criticism because it did
not fear it. He liked the curve of her neck and
the way it sat upon her shoulders, and the waves
of her heavy yellow hair. Her stories bored him.
But it seemed to him, now that it was written
that he was not to appreciate his good angels, he
must make the most of his bad angels, and this
one was no worse nor no better than the rest, and
she was certainly wonderfully good to look at.
"If you are ready," he said, "we will take the
coffee in the other room." He brought it and the
liqueurs in himself, and sent his man down-stairs.
It was a darkly furnished room, lit by candles
under red shades, and strewn with furs and heavy
rugs. It was part of the ideal apartments of a
young Englishman, from whom Thorold rented
it while the owner was off yachting, and it was
filled with the relics of his former voyages and the
tributes of bazaars and bric-à-brac shops. There
were great divans heaped with cushions, and huge
leather chairs, and arms, and rows of miniatures,
and blue and white saucers, and cabinets of ivory
from India filled with old silver and pretty trifles
from the Paris shops; and the smart dinner gowns

10

of the women as they moved from cabinet to picture, exclaiming over the treasures of the room,
gave to it just the life and color it most needed.

Cathcart sank into one of the big leather chairs
with a sigh of content. "Jolly sort of place this,
Thorold," he said.

Mrs. Inness poured out some brandy for herself, but Miss Gwynn went back to the dining-
room, and returned carrying the champagne in
its bucket, and placed it beside her on the floor.

"This is Liberty Hall, is it not?" she said. "I
fancied so. You'd better tell your man to have
some more of this ready. The captain and I
like it."

When Thorold returned, Mrs. Inness was at the
piano playing the *pas de quatre* from the Gaiety,
and Miss Gwynn was holding her skirts daintily
and dancing in the centre of the room. Cathcart
laughed from the recesses of the big chair.

"I tell her it's a shame she doesn't go on the
stage, Thorold. She can dance as well as Lind
or Sylvia Grey now, and she's only had five
lessons."

Mrs. Inness rose from the piano in apparent confusion. "I don't know what Mr. Thorold will
think of our taking possession in this way," she
exclaimed.

"Oh, don't stop," said the American. "It's
very pretty."

But the woman refused. She confessed to an
awe of her host which she could not explain, and

which troubled her in consequence. She could not understand him.

Thorold rolled up some of the rugs, leaving a bare place on the floor, and sitting down before the piano, began a Spanish bolero, to which the model danced, after a moment's hesitation, with a pretty recklessness that left her panting, and called out a round of applause.

"That was very good indeed," Thorold said.

"It makes me dry," the girl answered. "Did you see about that champagne?"

She went over to one of the little Turkish tables and took a cigarette from a box and lit it, blowing the smoke away with a laugh of content. Thorold handed the box to Mrs. Inness, but she shook her head.

"Oh, go on, Mildred. Don't be stiff," said Miss Gwynn. "We're all friends here."

"Yes, Mrs. Inness," Thorold repeated, "we're all friends here."

He smiled grimly at this as he walked back into the dining-room for the champagne. He was distinctly conscious that he was not having a good time. He argued that this was so because the impressions of the afternoon still hung upon him, and that when they had worn away he would be in a more appreciative mood. He congratulated himself that there would be no more such scenes in the future. Still, he was annoyed that his guests, whom he himself had selected, should enjoy themselves and that he should not. He assured himself that it was not the twenty-five years of virtue that was asserting itself, but that it was simply because the people were vulgar that they were unattractive. He paused for a moment in the darkened room with the bottle in his hand, trying to analyze what it was that was wrong in him. From the other room, beyond the portière, came the pop of a soda-water bottle, and Miss Gwynn's shrill laugh and Cathcart's comfortable bass. They seemed to be making themselves very much at home.

"What a prig I am!" Thorold said, impatiently. He decided swiftly that he was much too superior a person, and that if he meant to enjoy his new freedom he must crush the rising protests of past tastes and traditions and give himself to the present. He came into the room smiling.

"Sing us something, Miss Gwynn," he said.

Miss Gwynn demurred, shyly. "I wouldn't dare, before you," she said ; and then, to show how little she meant this, she sat down and ran her fingers over the keys of the piano. "I'll sing you something of Ivette Guilbert's," she said, over her shoulder. "My French is beastly, but I have to sing them in French, so that Cathcart won't understand."

"Oh, don't, Trix," said Mrs. Inness. "They're so low."

Thorold caught himself smiling at this, and to find that Mrs. Inness had her own ideas of propriety. Then he corrected himself mentally for

still criticising and posing as a superior being.
He was sick and disgusted with it all and with
himself. The girl at the piano was singing with
none of Guilbert's innocence of manner, but was
giving each line its full meaning. Mrs. Inness
laughed, and looked consciously at the floor;
Cathcart approved doubtfully, and suggested as
a compromise a song from the music-halls.

"No," said Miss Gwynn; "I've been funny
long enough. Let Thorold play something. I
want to be audience now."

"Oh, *do*, Mr. Thorold," said Mrs. Inness, effu-
sively.

"Play us a lot of things," said the model—
"the things you play to the swells."

Cathcart scrambled out of the arm-chair. "I
say, Thorold," he said, "if you wouldn't mind,
I'd like it awfully if you'd sing that 'Well of
Truth.' I'd like to hear you do it yourself. I'd
like to say I'd heard you."

Every instinct and taste of which Thorold was
possessed was offended and rose in rebellion as
they spoke to him. He hated them, and he hated
himself for having brought them to this room.
The wickedness of Mayfair and not of Bohemia,
he determined, would be his dissipation in the
future. He could at least choose his associates,
as heretofore, and he was not unmindful that
there were those of his own class a little more
wicked than Mrs. Inness, if not so beautiful.
"What a child I am!" he exclaimed. He reit-

erated to himself that he had chosen his own
way. The best and strongest help for good that
had ever come into his life had, so he believed,
failed him, had ceased to move him that very day;
and he thought, in his inexperience, that what he
needed now was to make going back, or the
thought of going back, an impossibility.

And then there came to him an inspiration.
In the three months in which the Puritan conscience and the artistic temperament had been
struggling for the mastery he had written and
composed the music for a song. He called it
" The Days that are Gone." The song was the
expression of all that had been going on in his
mind ; it meant to him the story of what he had
gone through, and through which he was still
going—all that he had lost, all his doubts, and
regret for what was lost. He had not sung it to
any one. He had even locked the doors when he
sang it alone ; for it had been written when he
was feeling more deeply than he had ever felt
before, and he guarded it for that reason, even
while his artistic judgment assured him that it
was, as a work of art, the strongest thing he had
ever written. It seemed to him now that if he
could bring himself to sing that song to these
people he would shame the best that was in him
and the best that had ever come from him, that
he would mock the thing that meant most to
him, and that if he cast it before these swine no
other sentiment or principle or tradition of his life

could lay claim to recognition. He turned impulsively towards his guests, smiling strangely.

"I want you to hear a new song I've written.
It's not a funny song ; it's rather the other way.
It's about some one, a man or a woman, who —
However, I'll sing it, and then you'll know what
it's about. I'll sing you some funny ones after I
have finished it."

There was a murmur of delighted interest, and
a rustle of silks as the women settled themselves
to listen.

"Wait till I get a light, will you ?" said Cathcart. He reached out of the recesses of the chair,
and leaning forward to one of the little tables,
struck a match.

Thorold placed his own cigar carefully on the
glass rim of one of the candles beside the music-
rack, and, as he waited, turned a smiling countenance upon his audience. The soldier's red-
bronzed face was showing in the light of the
flaring wax ; it was content, and marked with
pleasurable anticipation. On the floor at his side
Miss Gwynn had thrown one of the cushions,
and had seated herself upon it, leaning her head
against the arm of Cathcart's chair. She smiled
up brightly at Thorold as he looked at her, and
posed herself in an attitude that might have been
titled "Expectancy" or "Waiting," as though
she felt the eye of the artist or of the camera
upon her. In the centre of the room Mrs. Inness
sat, or rather reclined, on the broad arm of one

of the big leather chairs, leaning back, with one bare arm thrown behind her head, and with the other holding a glass, which she rested lightly on her knee. Her attitude showed her figure and almost every line of her body, from the point of her slippered toe, with which she tapped the floor, to the top of her well-poised head. It was a graceful, indolent, and obviously meditated pose, which Thorold observed with cynical approval. The woman, catching his eye, raised the glass from her knee, and bent her head gracefully, smiling as she did so with half-closed eyes. Thorold laughed shortly, and struck the opening chord of his song. The words could have been sung by either a man or a woman. It began by telling of the days of the past, the days that were gone; and the accompaniment suggested the brightness of sunshine and of running streams and rustling leaves, of the "lost Eden of our innocence" and of sweet content; then it merged suddenly into braver and more powerful strains as the words spoke of ambitions and hopes and of great deeds for the life in the future.

Thorold had a very good voice, full of dramatic feeling and power, and every word he sang came to the listener's ear bearing its proper emphasis as sharp and sure as the lines of an actor's soliloquy.

He began contemptuously, but the artist in him made it impossible for him to do aught else but sing the song well. The music changed to low mutterings, and the words told of doubts and trouble, and then broke out into passionate regret and agony of spirit. One could almost see the beads of sweat upon the face of the suppliant. It was a cry for peace and rest, and return to the quiet streams and gentle shade. Thorold had forgotten himself and his audience. His voice rose and met the rising wail of the music; it told of wasted days, of unresting and feverish searchings for happiness and relief from thought, of the sting of dead desires, and of the mockery of pleasure. The music grew in volume, and filled the room with a great cry of mourning, eerie, awful, and despairing. Hopelessness and remorse were the meaning of the music and of the words —the impotent cry for the days that could not come again, the futile regret for the chances that had passed and that had not been taken; and then the voice of the singer sank and died away with one low deep cry, as though despairing of succor or relief, without faith and without hope, and the music running on ended in a wild crash that sounded like the laughter of those already lost, mocking at those just fallen. The room was strangely silent.

Thorold reached for his cigar and relit it at the candle. He puffed it back into a flame again, and then, as no one moved, turned slowly towards his guests. Cathcart sat just as he had last noticed him, leaning forward with the half-burned match still in his hand. He had not moved.

His shoulders were stooped, and he was staring out across the half-lit room with a pitiful, uncomprehending look in his eyes like that of a child in trouble. The fat fingers that held his cigar trembled on his knees.

The girl at his feet was staring up at Thorold with wide-open eyes, pleading and terrified. Her lips were quivering. And then as Thorold smiled she did the only natural thing she had ever done in her short, silly, artificial life, and, turning swiftly, threw herself across Cathcart's knees and burst into a wild torrent of tears.

Thorold sprang up with an exclamation that was half anger and half apology. He turned towards the older woman of the two for some explanation, and then sank back again slowly before the piano. Mrs. Inness had not altered her position, but the meaning, languishing smile was gone, and had changed to one of frank, open-eyed amusement. She was looking at him as though she had known him for a long time in the past, but as though he had but just then disclosed himself. Her awe of him that he himself had noticed earlier in the evening had fallen from her like a cloak, and she was smiling at him familiarly and with a look of perfect understanding and equality. Thorold turned away his eyes and struck the keys resentfully. What had this woman to do with him? Mrs. Inness rose leisurely, and swept smiling across the room towards him. She leaned one bare elbow on the piano,

"HOPELESSNESS AND REMORSE WERE THE MEANING OF THE MUSIC"

and placed the hand of the other arm on her hip
with the arm akimbo and her head thrown back.
In her right hand she he.d the glass, and with
the forefinger of the same hand she pointed at
Thorold. She was not a very tall woman, but
she seemed to tower above him as he sat looking
up at her, his fingers wandering over the keys.
Her attitude was too easy to be graceful, and to
Thorold it seemed to have a touch of menace in
it and of insolence. She nodded her head at him,
smiling strangely between half-closed eyelids.

"And you," she said at last, speaking slowly,
and smiling with each word, "you're Archibald
Thorold, are you? You're the man who wrote
'The Well of Truth,' and the oratorios, and those
operas the curates go to see. What a jolly fraud
you are!" She laughed easily, and touched the
glass to her lips, and then pushed it away from
her across the piano. "You're the man who writes
the songs the little girls cry over, all about Love
and the Ideal. Oh, I know! I've sung them and
cried over them, too. And now here you are, just
like anybody else — aren't you? Just an every-
day, common, ordinary *man*."

Thorold pressed heavily on the keys beneath
his fingers. "I do not think, Mrs. Inness," he
said, stiffly, "that I ever posed as being anything
else."

"Perhaps not," the woman went on, easily.
"Perhaps not. But *why* aren't you different?
Why are you just like all the other Johnnies?"

She rested her chin on the palm of her hand, and looked into his with frank, wide-open eyes. And yet Thorold doubted her frankness, and looked up at her uneasily.

"I don't think I understand you," he said, with severe politeness.

"Oh yes, you do," she laughed, lightly. "You *know* you're not like them. I don't mean your being a swell, but the rest of it." She turned and pointed her hand towards the corner where Cathcart sat in the semi-darkness patting the girl's curls as they rested on his knee. She had sobbed herself to sleep, or was pretending to sleep, and the man was puffing softly on his cigar and looking down at her. "You see," said Mrs. Inness, "if you're able to make Cathcart look as though he had seen a ghost, and to send Beatrice Gwynn off into hysterics with remorse, you must be different from most Johnnies. And you've made me cry many a time. And I know a girl, a sick girl, down in Kent. I used to play and sing your songs to her when I was down there, and she—well!—*she* thinks you're a gilded saint."

"Drop it, will you!" Thorold said. He half rose from the chair, but the woman touched him familiarly on the shoulder and pushed him down.

"No; you listen to me," she said. Her eyes were brilliant, and she had ceased smiling. "I want to talk to you; I've wanted to know you for a long time. Why," she said, laughing uneasily, "I've got a dozen pictures of you in my house

now: I sent to the States for them.   Yes, I did;
and I'm no more keen about you than a lot more
of other women I know.   I've thought if I could
meet a man like you—I mean, you know," she explained, "the sort of man I thought you were—
that things would be better, or worse, for it.   You
see," she said, laughing unmirthfully, "you never
know just who *is* counting on you in this world—
do you?   A chap like you has responsibilities;
but you're quite right to shove them over.   You
have a livelier time, I fancy—don't you?—than
if you bothered with them."   She stopped and
looked down, with her lips pressed together, and
breathing heavily.   "But it's hard on the others
sometimes — on that sick girl I was telling you
about, for instance.   I guess if she knew, it would
about kill *her*.   And it's hard on me."   Thorold's
cigar was out, and the candles on either side of the
piano had sunk to their sockets, and were sputtering in wavering, uncertain flashes.   "That's what
you did for me," the woman went on, bitterly.
Her voice chilled Thorold as it came from above
like the falling of cold rain upon his bare head.
"I counted on you," she said.   "I used to think
that as long as there was one man left who believed in us we weren't so bad, that there was a
chance of our getting better or our getting back.
I've sung those songs of yours, and they sort of
comforted me.   They made me feel there was
something good in me too, and I could have loved
the man who made me feel that, the man who

wrote those songs, if I had met him. I could
have done anything for him—anything. I'd have
been — different for him if he had wanted me
to, and now—now I can't." Her voice had risen
suddenly, but she lowered it again into a sharp,
fierce whisper. "I can't. Now that I've met
you I can't. I wish I'd never seen you. I'd
rather be a fool, believing there was one man who
was different—different from all the rest of you.
I hate you!" she whispered; "I hate you! I'd
made so much of you. I counted on you so, and
you're no better than Cathcart there — not so
good, for he doesn't preach one thing and live
another. He doesn't pretend to be any better
than he is—and you, oh! you—you don't want to
be as good as you are. You've fooled them all—
haven't you? You've been very clever. Aren't
you pleased with it? Aren't you proud?" Her
voice broke with a sob, and she turned swiftly
away and swept out of the room into the hall beyond.

Thorold sat quite motionless. His head was
bent, and his fingers still rested on the silent keys.
All he had ever said to himself, or all that others
had said to him, had never come to him as had
the words of this woman, whose name was "as
common as the Paris road," and whom he had de-
spised himself for admiring, even while he pitied
her. He was sore, bruised, and sick, as though he
had been pelted with stones and pointed at on a
pillory. Outside, the birds in the Park across the

street were chirping violently, and the early sun
came stealing between the cracks of the blinds
into the smoke-laden room.

Thorold rose stiffly and uncertainly, as though
he had been sitting there a very long time, and
followed her.

A tall white figure, muffled and unrecognizable,
confronted him in the gray half-light of the hall.
" Well ?" she said.

Thorold went to the door and threw it open, letting in the sunlight, and giving them a strangely
foreign and unfamiliar air. It was as if the night
just over were far back in the past.

" Mrs. Inness," he said, " you won't understand
me, I am afraid. But I want you to know that,
though I have disappointed you, you have helped
me a great deal. I think I owe it to you to tell
you this. We never know, as you say, how much
we depend on others, and we can never tell from
what source that help we most need will come."

" I don't understand," the woman said.

" Never mind," Thorold answered, gently. " It
is something that you have helped another, is it
not ?"

Cathcart and the girl came into the hall, and
Cathcart stepped into the street and beckoned to
the line of hansoms drawn up by the railings under the overhanging branches of the Park.

" I'm sorry I made such an ass of myself, Thorold," the soldier said, " but that song of yours
was a bit creepy, now, wasn't it ?"

The model stretched a slim white hand out from the mass of swan's-down, and as Thorold took it in his own, she stooped and kissed his hand, and then ran down the steps, laughing, to where Cathcart stood waiting beside the hansom. Thorold helped Mrs. Inness into the next, and gave her number to the driver, but she called to him to wait. She pushed the doors away and leaned forward, gathering the cloak up about her bare throat.

"You are angry with me," she said. Her eyes were wet and pleading. "You will never forgive me. I don't know why I spoke as I did. I was a fool—because I don't want you to hate me. I want you to forgive me, and come to see me, in spite of all I said."

"There is nothing to forgive, Mrs. Inness," Thorold answered, earnestly. "I tell you, you have done me a great service. You have helped me very much."

"Oh, I know," she interrupted, impatiently. "You say that, but you are angry. Don't think of what I said. Forget it and forgive me, and come and see me."

Thorold smiled. He could not help it, for the way seemed so clear now.

"I am very sorry," he said, "but really I can't. You see, I'm leaving town. I sail for America this morning with some friends from Southampton."

The woman sank back against the cushions,

with her face hid from him in the high collar of
her cloak. Thorold stood motionless upon the
curb, watching the hansom as it swept away,
echoing down the empty, sunlit street. When it
had disappeared, he turned slowly and walked
back soberly into the darkened rooms. The candles were still burning, and the empty bottles and
the ashes of half-burned cigars lay scattered over
the floor and tables. Thorold opened the blinds,
letting in the sunlight upon the disorder and dé-
bris of the night just over. He surveyed the room
curiously, and for the last time. "And it was
here," he said, gravely, "that I entertained an
angel unawares."

THE BOY ORATOR OF ZEPATA CITY

THE day was cruelly hot, with unwarranted gusts of wind which swept the red dust in fierce eddies in at one end of Main Street and out at the other, and waltzed fantastically across the prairie. When they had passed, human beings opened their eyes again to blink hopelessly at the white sun, and swore or gasped, as their nature moved them. There were very few human beings in the streets, either in Houston Avenue, where there were dwelling-houses, or in the business quarter on Main Street. They were all at the new court-house, and every one possessed of proper civic pride was either in the packed court-room itself, or standing on the high steps outside, or pacing the long, freshly kalsomined corridors, where there was shade and less dust. It was an eventful day in the history of Zepata City. The court-house had been long in coming, the appropriation had been denied again and again; but at last it stood a proud and hideous fact, like a gray prison, towering above the bare, undecorated brick stores and the frame houses on the prairie around it, new, raw, and cheap, from the tin statue on the dome to the stucco round its base already cracking with the sun.   Piles of lumber and scaffolding and the lime beds the builders had left still lay on the unsodded square, and the bursts of wind drove the shavings across it, as they had done since the first day of building, when the Hon. Horatio Macon, who had worked for the appropriation, had laid the corner-stone and received the homage of his constituents.

It seemed a particularly happy and appropriate circumstance that the first business in the new court-room should be of itself of an important and momentous nature, something that dealt not only with the present but with the past of Zepata, and that the trial of so celebrated an individual as Abe Barrow should open the court-house with *éclat*, as Emma Abbott, who had come all the way from San Antonio to do it, had opened the new opera-house the year before.   The District Attorney had said it would not take very long to dispose of Barrow's case, but he had promised it would be an interesting if brief trial, and the court-room was filled even to the open windows, where men sat crowded together, with the perspiration running down their faces, and the red dust settling and turning white upon their shoulders.

Abe Barrow, the prisoner, had been as closely associated with the early history of Zepata as Colonel Macon himself, and was as widely known; he had killed in his day several of the Zepata citizens, and two visiting brother-desperadoes, and the corner where his gambling-house had stood was still known as Barrow's Corner, to the regret

of the druggist who had opened a shop there.
Ten years before, the murder of Deputy-Sheriff
Welsh had led him to the penitentiary, and a
month previous to the opening of the new court-
house he had been freed, and arrested at the prison
gate to stand trial for the murder of Hubert
Thompson. The fight with Thompson had been
a fair fight — so those said who remembered it —
and Thompson was a man they could well spare;
but the case against Barrow had been prepared
during his incarceration by the new and youthful
District Attorney, "Judge" Henry Harvey, and
as it offered a fitting sacrifice for the dedication
of the new temple of justice, the people were satisfied and grateful.

The court-room was as bare of ornament as the
cell from which the prisoner had just been taken.
There was an imitation walnut clock at the back
of the Judge's hair-cloth sofa, his revolving chair,
and his high desk. This was the only ornament.
Below was the green table of the District Attorney, upon which rested his papers and law-books
and his high hat. To one side sat the jury, ranch-
owners and prominent citizens, proud of having to
serve on this the first day; and on the other the
prisoner in his box. Around them gathered the
citizens of Zepata in close rows, crowded together
on unpainted benches; back of them more citizens
standing and a few awed Mexicans; and around
all the whitewashed walls. Colonel John Stogart,
of Dallas, the prisoner's attorney, procured obvi-

ously at great expense, no one knew by whom, and Barrow's wife, a thin yellow-faced woman in a mean-fitting showy gown, sat among the local celebrities at the District Attorney's elbow. She was the only woman in the room.

Colonel Stogart's speech had been good. The citizens were glad it had been so good; it had kept up the general tone of excellence, and it was well that the best lawyer of Dallas should be present on this occasion, and that he should have made what the citizens of Zepata were proud to believe was one of the efforts of his life. As they said, a court-house such as this one was not open for business every day. It was also proper that Judge Truax, who was a real Judge, and not one by courtesy only, as was the young District Attorney, should sit upon the bench. He also was associated with the early days and with the marvellous growth of Zepata City. He had taught the young District Attorney much of what he knew, and his long white hair and silver-rimmed spectacles gave dignity and the appearance of calm justice to the bare room and to the heated words of the rival orators.

Colonel Stogart ceased speaking, and the District Attorney sucked in his upper lip with a nervous impatient sigh as he recognized that the visiting attorney had proved murder in the second degree, and that an execution in the jail-yard would not follow as a fitting sequence.

But he was determined that so far as in him lay

he would at least send his man back to the penitentiary for the remainder of his life.

Young Harry Harvey, "The Boy Orator of
Zepata City," as he was called, was very dear to
the people of that booming town. In their eyes
he was one of the most promising young men in
the whole great unwieldy State of Texas, and the
boy orator thought they were probably right, but
he was far too clever to let them see it. He was
clever in his words and in his deeds and in his appearance. And he dressed much more carefully
than any other man in town, with a frock-coat and
a white tie winter and summer, and a fine high hat.
That he was slight and short of stature was something he could not help, and was his greatest,
keenest regret, and that Napoleon was also short
and slight did not serve to satisfy him or to make
his regret less continual. What availed the sharply
cut, smoothly shaven face and the eyes that flashed
when he was moved, or the bell-like voice, if every
unlettered ranchman or ranger could place both
hands on his shoulders and look down at him from
heights above? But they forgot this and he forgot it before he had reached the peroration of his
closing speech. They saw only the Harry Harvey
they knew and adored moving and rousing them
with his voice, trembling with indignation when
he wished to tremble, playing all his best tricks
in his best manner, and cutting the air with sharp,
cruel words when he was pleased to be righteously
just.

The young District Attorney turned slowly on his heels, and swept the court-room carelessly with a glance of the clever black eyes. The moment was his. He saw all the men he knew—the men who made his little world—crowding silently forward, forgetful of the heat, of the suffocating crush of those about them, of the wind that rattled the doors in the corridors, and conscious only of him. He saw his old preceptor watching keenly from the bench, with a steady glance of perfect appreciation, such as that with which one actor in the box compliments the other on the stage. He saw the rival attorney—the great lawyer from the great city—nervously smiling, with a look of confidence that told the lack of it; and he saw the face of the prisoner grim and set and hopelessly defiant. The boy orator allowed his uplifted arm to fall until the fingers pointed at the prisoner.

"This man," he said, and as he spoke even the wind in the corridors hushed for the moment, "is no part or parcel of Zepata City of to-day. He comes to us a relic of the past—a past that has brought honor to many, wealth to some, and which is dear to all of us who love the completed purpose of their work ; a past that was full of hardships and glorious efforts in the face of daily disappointments, embitterments, and rebuffs. But the part *this* man played in that past lives only in the rude court records of that day, in the traditions of the gambling-hell and the saloons, and on the head-stones of his victims. He was one of

the excrescences of that unsettled period, an un-
happy evil — an inevitable evil, I might almost
say, as the Mexican horse-thieves and the prairie
fires and the Indian outbreaks were inevitable, as
our fathers who built this beautiful city knew to
their cost. The same chance that was given to
them to make a home for themselves in the wilderness, to help others to make their homes, to
assist the civilization and progress not only of
this city, but of the whole Lone Star State, was
given to him, and he refused it, and blocked the
way of others, and kept back the march of progress, until to-day, civilization, which has waxed
great and strong—not on account of him, remember, but in spite of him — sweeps him out of its
way, and crushes him and his fellows."

The young District Attorney allowed his arm
to drop, and turned to the jury, leaning easily
with his bent knuckles on the table.

"Gentlemen," he said, in his pleasant tones of
every-day politeness, "the 'bad man' has become
an unknown quantity in Zepata City and in the
State of Texas. It lies with you to see that he
remains so. He went out of existence with the
blanket Indian and the buffalo. He is dead, and
he must *not* be resurrected. He was a picturesque
evil of those early days, but civilization has no
use for him, and it has killed him, as the railroads
and the barb - wire fence have killed the cowboy.
He does not belong here; he does not fit in; he is
not wanted. We want men who can breed good

cattle, who can build manufactories and open banks; storekeepers who can undersell those of other cities; and professional men who know their business. We do *not* want desperadoes and 'bad men' and faro-dealers and men who are quick on the trigger. A foolish and morbid publicity has cloaked men of this class with a notoriety which cheap and pernicious literature has greatly helped to disseminate. They have been made romantic when they were brutal, brave when they were foolhardy, heroes when they were only bullies and blackguards. This man, Abe Barrow, the prisoner at the bar, belongs to that class. He enjoys and has enjoyed a reputation as a 'bad man,' a desperate and brutal ruffian. Free him to-day, and you set a premium on such reputations; acquit him of this crime, and you encourage others to like evil. Let him go, and he will walk the streets with a swagger, and boast that you were afraid to touch him — *afraid*, gentlemen — and children and women will point after him as the man who has sent nine others into eternity, and who yet walks the streets a free man. And he will become, in the eyes of the young and the weak, a hero and a god. This is unfortunate, but it is true.

"Now, gentlemen, we want to keep the streets of this city so safe that a woman can walk them at midnight without fear of insult, and a man can express his opinion on the corner without being shot in the back for doing so."

The District Attorney turned from the jury with a bow, and faced Judge Truax.

"For the last ten years, your honor, this man, Abner Barrow, has been serving a term of imprisonment in the State penitentiary; I ask you to send him back there again for the remainder of his life. It will be the better place for him, and we will be happier in knowing we have done our duty in placing him there. Abe Barrow is out of date. He has missed step with the march of progress, and has been out of step for ten years, and it is best for all that he should remain out of it until he, who has sent nine other men unprepared to meet their God—"

"He is not on trial for the murder of nine men," interrupted Colonel Stogart, springing from his chair, "but for the justifiable killing of one, and I demand, your honor, that—"

"—has sent nine other men to meet their Maker," continued the District Attorney, "meets with the awful judgment of a higher court than this."

Colonel Stogart smiled scornfully at the platitude, and sat down with an expressive shrug; but no one noticed him.

The District Attorney raised his arm and faced the court-room. "It cannot be said of *us*," he cried, "that we have sat idle in the market-place. We have advanced and advanced in the last ten years, until we have reached the very foremost place with civilized people. This Rip Van Winkle of the past returns to find a city where he left a prairie town, a bank where he spun his roulette wheel, this magnificent court-house instead of a vigilance committee. And what is his part in this new court-house, which to-day, for the first time, throws open its doors to protect the just and to punish the unjust?

"Is he there in the box among those honorable men, the gentlemen of the jury? Is he in that great crowd of intelligent, public-spirited citizens who make the bone and sinew of this our fair city? Is he on the honored bench dispensing justice, and making the intricacies of the law straight? No, gentlemen; he has no part in our triumph. He is there, in the prisoners' pen, an outlaw, a convicted murderer, and an unconvicted assassin, the last of his race—the bullies and bad men of the border—a thing to be forgotten and put away forever from the sight of man. He has outlasted his time; he is a superfluity and an outrage on our reign of decency and order. And I ask you, gentlemen, to put him away where he will not hear the voice of man nor children's laughter, nor see a woman smile, where he will not even see the face of the warden who feeds him, nor sunlight except as it is filtered through the iron bars of a jail. Bury him with the bitter past, with the lawlessness that has gone— that has gone, thank God—and which must *not* return. Place him in the cell where he belongs, and whence, had justice been done, he would never have been taken alive."

The District Attorney sat down suddenly, with a quick nod to the Judge and the jury, and fumbled over his papers with nervous fingers. He was keenly conscious, and excited with the fervor of his own words. He heard the reluctantly hushed applause and the whispers of the crowd, and noted the quick and combined movement of the jury with a selfish sweet pleasure, which showed itself only in the tightening of the lips and nostrils. Those nearest him tugged at his sleeve and shook hands with him. He remembered this afterwards as one of the rewards of the moment. He turned the documents before him over and scribbled words upon a piece of paper and read a passage in an open law-book. He did this quite mechanically, and was conscious of nothing until the foreman pronounced the prisoner at the bar guilty of murder in the second degree.

Judge Truax leaned across his desk and said, simply, that it lay in his power to sentence the prisoner to not less than two years' confinement in the State penitentiary or for the remainder of his life.

"Before I deliver sentence on you, Abner Barrow," he said, with an old man's kind severity, "is there anything you have to say on your own behalf?"

The District Attorney turned his face, as did all the others, but he did not see the prisoner. He still saw himself holding the court-room with

a spell, and heard his own periods ringing against
the whitewashed ceiling. The others saw a tall,
broad-shouldered man leaning heavily forward
over the bar of the prisoner's box. His face was
white with the prison tan, markedly so in contrast with those sunburnt by the wind and sun
turned towards him, and pinched and hollow-
eyed and worn. When he spoke, his voice had
the huskiness which comes from non-use, and
cracked and broke like a child's.

"I don't know, Judge," he said, hesitatingly,
and staring stupidly at the mass of faces in the
well beneath him, "that I have anything to say—
in my own behalf. I don't know as it would be
any use. I guess what the gentleman said about
me is all there is to say. He put it about right.
I've had my fun, and I've got to pay for it—that
is, I thought it was fun at the time. I am not
going to cry any baby act and beg off, or anything, if that's what you mean. But there is
something I'd like to say if I thought you would
believe me." He frowned down at the green table as though the words he wanted would not
come, and his eyes wandered from one face to
another, until they rested upon the bowed head
of the only woman in the room. They remained
there for some short time, and then Barrow drew
in his breath more quickly, and turned with something like a show of confidence to the jury.

"All that man said of me is true," he said. He
gave a toss of his hands as a man throws away

the reins. "I admit all he says. I *am* a back number; I *am* out of date; I *was* a loafer and a blackguard. I never shot any man in the back, nor I never assassinated no one; but that's neither here nor there. I'm not in a place where I can expect people to pick out their words; but, as he says, I *am* a bad lot. He says I have enjoyed a reputation as a desperado. I am not bragging of that; I just ask you to remember that he said it. Remember it of me. I was not the sort to back down to man or beast, and I'm not now. I am not backing down now; I'm taking my punishment. Whatever you please to make it, I'll take it; and that," he went on, more slowly, "makes it harder for me to ask what I want to ask, and make you all believe I am not asking it for myself."

He stopped, and the silence in the room seemed to give him some faint encouragement of sympathy, though it was rather the silence of curiosity.

Colonel Stogart gave a stern look upward, and asked the prisoner's wife, in a whisper, if she knew what her husband meant to say, but she shook her head. She did not know. The District Attorney smiled indulgently at the prisoner and at the men about him, but they were watching the prisoner.

"That man there," said Barrow, pointing with one gaunt hand at the boy attorney, "told you I had no part or parcel in this city or in this

world ; that I belonged to the past; that I had
ought to be dead. Now that's not so. I have
just one thing that belongs to this city and this
world—and to me; one thing that I couldn't take
to jail with me, and that I'll have to leave behind
me when I go back to it. I mean my wife."

The prisoner stopped, and looked so steadily at
one place below him that those in the back of the
court guessed for the first time that Mrs. Barrow
was in the room, and craned forward to look at
her, and there was a moment of confusion and a
murmur of "Get back there!" "Sit still!" The
prisoner turned to Judge Truax again and squared
his broad shoulders, making the more conspicuous
his narrow and sunken chest.

"You, sir," he said, quietly, with a change from
the tone of braggadocio with which he had begun
to speak, "remember her, sir, when I married
her, twelve years ago. She was Henry Holman's
daughter, he who owned the San Iago Ranch and
the triangle brand. I took her from the home
she had with her father against that gentleman's
wishes, sir, to live with me over my dance-hall at
the Silver Star. You may remember her as she
was then. She gave up everything a woman
ought to have to come to me. She thought she
was going to be happy with me ; that's why she
come, I guess. Maybe she was happy for about
two weeks. After that first two weeks her life,
sir, was a hell, and I made it a hell. I was drunk
most of the time, or sleeping it off, and ugly-

tempered when I was sober. There was shooting and carrying on all day and night down-stairs, and she didn't dare to leave her room. Besides that, she cared for me, and she was afraid every minute I was going to get killed. That's the way she lived for two years. Respectable women wouldn't speak to her because she was my wife; even them that were friends of hers when she lived on the ranch wouldn't speak to her on the street—and she had no children. That was her life; she lived alone over the dance-hall; and sometimes when I was drunk—I beat her."

The man's white face reddened slowly as he said this; and he stopped, and then continued more quickly, with his eyes still fixed on those of the Judge:

"At the end of two years I killed Welsh, and they sent me to the penitentiary for ten years, and she was free. She could have gone back to her folks and got a divorce if she'd wanted to, and never seen me again. It was an escape most women 'd gone down on their knees and thanked their Maker for, and blessed the day they'd been freed from a blackguardly drunken brute.

"But what did this woman do—my wife, the woman I misused and beat and dragged down in the mud with me? She was too mighty proud to go back to her people or to the friends who shook her when she was in trouble; and she sold out the place, and bought a ranch with the money, and worked it by herself, worked it day and night, until in ten years she had made herself an old woman, as you see she is to-day.

"And for what? To get *me* free again; to bring *me* things to eat in jail, and picture papers and tobacco—when she was living on bacon and potatoes, and drinking alkali water—working to pay for a lawyer to fight for *me*—to pay for the *best* lawyer! She worked in the fields with her own hands, planting and ploughing, working as I never worked for myself in my whole lazy, rotten life. That's what that woman there did for me."

The man stopped suddenly, and turned with a puzzled look towards where his wife sat, for she had dropped her head on the table in front of her, and he had heard her sobbing.

"And what I want to ask of you, sir, is to let me have two years out of jail to show her how I feel about it. I ask you not to send me back for life, sir. Give me just two years—two years of my life while I have some strength left to work for her as she worked for me. I only want to show her how I care for her *now*. I had the chance, and I wouldn't take it; and now, sir, I want to show her that I know and understand—now, when it's too late. It's all I've thought of when I was in jail, to be able to see her sitting in her own kitchen with her hands folded, and me working and sweating in the fields for her—working till every bone ached, trying to make it up to her.

"And I can't!" the man cried, suddenly, losing

the control he had forced upon himself, and tossing his hands up above his head, and with his eyes fixed hopelessly on the bowed head below him. "I can't! It's too late. It's too late!"

He turned and faced the crowd and the District Attorney defiantly.

"I'm not crying for the men I killed. They're dead. I can't bring them back. But she's not dead, and I treated her worse than I treated them. *She* never harmed me, nor got in my way, nor angered me. And now, when I want to do what I can for her in the little time that's left, *he* tells you I'm a 'relic of the past,' that civilization's too good for me, that you must bury me until it's time to bury me for good. Just when I've got something I *must* live for, something I've got to do. Don't you believe me? Don't you understand?"

He turned again towards the Judge, and beat the rail before him impotently with his wasted hand. "Don't send me back for life!" he cried. "Give me a few years to work for her—two years, one year—to show her what I feel here, what I never felt for her before. Look at her, gentlemen. Look how worn she is and poorly, and look at her hands, and you men must feel how I feel. I don't ask you for myself. I don't want to go free on my own account. I am asking it for that woman—yes, and for myself, too. I am playing to 'get back,' gentlemen. I've lost what I had, and I want to get back; and," he cried, queru-

"THE GENTLEMEN OF THE JURY SAT QUITE MOTIONLESS"

lously, "the game keeps going against me. It's
only a few years' freedom I want. Send me back
for thirty years, but not for life. My God! Judge,
don't bury me alive, as that man asked you to.
I'm *not* civilized, maybe ; ways *have* changed.
You are not the man I knew ; you are all strangers to me. But I could learn. I wouldn't
bother you in the old way. I only want to live
with her. I won't harm the rest of you. Give
me this last chance. Let me prove that what I'm
saying is true."

The man stopped and stood, opening and shut-
ting his hands upon the rail, and searching with
desperate eagerness from face to face, as one who
has staked all he has watches the wheel spinning
his fortune away. The gentlemen of the jury sat
quite motionless, looking straight ahead at the
blinding sun, which came through the high un-
curtained windows opposite. Outside, the wind
banged the shutters against the wall, and whistled
up the street and round the tin corners of the
building, but inside, the room was very silent.
The Mexicans at the door, who could not understand, looked curiously at the faces of the men
around them, and made sure that they had missed
something of much importance. For a moment
no one moved, until there was a sudden stir around
the District Attorney's table, and the men stepped
aside and let the woman pass them and throw
herself against the prisoner's box. The prisoner
bent his tall gaunt figure over the rail, and as the

woman pressed his one hand against her face, touched her shoulders with the other awkwardly.

"There, now," he whispered, soothingly, "don't you take on so. Now you know how I feel, it's all right; don't take on."

Judge Truax looked at the paper on his desk for some seconds, and raised his head, coughing as he did so. "It lies—" Judge Truax began, and then stopped, and began again, in a more certain tone : "It lies at the discretion of this Court to sentence the prisoner to a term of imprisonment of two years, or for an indefinite period, or for life. Owing to— On account of certain circumstances which were—have arisen—this sentence is suspended. This court stands adjourned."

As he finished he sprang out of his chair impulsively, and with a quick authoritative nod to the young District Attorney, came quickly down the steps of the platform. Young Harvey met him at the foot with wide-open eyes.

The older man hesitated, and placed his hand upon the District Attorney's shoulder. "Harry," he said. His voice was shaken, and his hand trembled on the arm of his protégé, for he was an old man and easily moved. "Harry, my boy," he said, "do you think you could go to Austin and repeat the speech that man made to the Governor?"

The boy orator laughed, and took one of the older man's hands in one of his and pressed it quickly. "I'd like d——d well to try," he said.

THE ROMANCE IN THE LIFE OF HEFTY BURKE

HEFTY BURKE was a young man of honest countenance and godlike figure, who had been born by some mischance in the Fourth Ward, instead of in a more exclusive neighborhood, where he would later in life have been able to show off the godlike figure in a frock-coat. Having been born on the East River front, he had followed the river for a livelihood ever since, and could swim when other children of his age were learning to walk about alone. This fact had been demonstrated only by accident, but was vouched for by those who had seen him at the age of three jump out of his father's arms over the railing of an excursion-boat, and paddle around in the water until dragged out of it at the end of a boat-hook.

At the age of twenty-five he was making small sums of money by backing himself to win in swimming races, and had been given numerous medals for saving life. This latter recreation he regarded only as a divertisement. He did not make a business of it, and it was not to him a matter of serious moment, like the winning of long-distance championships. But neither of these

performances made him wealthy, and it was most
necessary that he should become so in order that
he might marry Miss Mary Casey, the daughter
of the janitor of the Mount Blanc Flats. Hefty
was very much in love with her, and had urged
her to marry him and live on the little money
he could earn, but Miss Casey was a thoughtful
young person, and thoroughly appreciated her own
value. She wished him to show his love by ap-
preciating it also. It is sometimes difficult to
express the magnitude of one's love by one's
wages, and Hefty found this true, but Miss Casey
saw no excuse in it. They had been engaged for
over a year.

But while it was difficult for him to earn money,
it was as easy for him to drag a drowning man
from death to the pier-head as for you to guide a
blind man from one sidewalk to the other, or a
girl across a ballroom; and his manner in doing
the one thing was as matter-of-fact, and as little
self-conscious, as yours would probably be in per-
forming the other. If the drowning person struggled, he ducked her, if it chanced to be a woman;
or, if it were a man, drew away an arm's-length
and trod water until he had posed his victim properly, when he would strike him once between the
eyes, and then slip him over his shoulder like a
bag of meal, and sweep in with him to a firm
mooring.

There was not, accordingly, the least hesitation
in the movements of Mr. Burke when the daughter

of Señor Juan Alvarez failed to place her foot on
the lower rung of the accommodation-ladder, and
sank between the port side of the tramp steamer
Liverpool and the *Liverpool's* long-boat. There
was no one left in the *Liverpool's* long-boat to
go after her, because her father, who had rowed
it over from the slip, had mounted the ship's ladder first, and was trying to balance himself on it,
and at the same time hold the long-boat back
against a turning tide that strove to wrench it
out of his hands. Mr. Burke was at this moment
tacking around the stern of the steamer in a cat-
boat. There was no time to go about and chase
the broad white hat that rose for an instant at
the foot of the ladder, so when he heard the father scream he dropped his sheet and tiller and
dived over the boat's rail to leeward, leaving her
reeling and careening impotently in the wind.
The broad straw hat rose once more at the steamer's bow and sank again, but Mr. Burke was in
close pursuit now, going hand after hand even
faster than the current, with his head under water,
and turning his mouth to the surface at each fifth
stroke to gasp for a breath of air. And when down
below him he saw, turning and twisting in the
sharp undercurrent, a slim white figure, he dived
for it and brought it up firmly under his arm, and
struck out confidently for the anchor-chain that
stretched above his head a few rods farther back,
quivering in the current. He reached it with a
few quick strokes, and threw his arm over it and

hung there, breathing heavily, and shaking the damp hair from his eyes. He saw the men of the *Liverpool* tumbling into the long-boat, and three tugs making towards him with fierce shrieks of their whistles, and the passengers on a lumbering ferry-boat crowded at the rail and pointing him out. It is almost as difficult to drown in the upper bay as in Madison Square, and Mr. Burke, knowing this, concerned himself not at all with the approaching aid, but turned his eyes with careless interest to the face beside his own. The broad straw hat had been wrenched away, and the long hair loosened, and the smooth oval face pressed against his was still warm through the water which ran from it. It was a different face from any which Mr. Burke had known. He would have classed its owner, had he been asked to give a guess at her nationality, as a foreigner, and more particularly as "Eyetalian," Italians being to him a generic term for all those people not born between the East and North rivers. But he admitted mentally that it was a very beautiful face. The lashes were longer than any he had ever seen, and the lips smaller, and the skin a warmer, browner tint, which made the clinched teeth under the parted lips more white by contrast. It reminded him of a picture he knew in the cathedral, but he could not recall just then where he had seen it. The face was so delicate and beautiful that he instinctively moved his own away from it, and relaxed his hold round the

girl's body, and as her head sank back on his
shoulder he gave a short laugh, and wondered
with a grim smile what Mary Casey would say if
she could see him then.   One of the men in the
long-boat lifted her up gently, and her father
seized her and caressed her and moaned and wept
over her, chattering in a soft unknown tongue.
Hefty had never before seen a man of his age
weep, and he observed it with interest, as he pulled
himself up over the bow of the boat.   The captain of one of the three tugs leaned over the low
rail and recognized Hefty with a wave of his
hand.

"I bet on it it was you," he said.   And then
added, looking down at his shoulder with a languishing smile, "Who's your friend?"

Mr. Burke reddened fiercely at this, and did not
answer; but whether he had blushed from anger
or embarrassment he could not tell.   He still felt
the touch of the girl's face against his own, and
as he became conscious of this, he rubbed his
cheek hastily with the back of his hand, as a
tribute of fidelity to Miss Casey, who had not
been there to see.

He sailed back to the slip in his recovered cat-
boat with a strange sensation of excitement and
unrest.   He had never felt excited when he had
saved other people, and he attributed his feeling
so at this time to the embarrassingly fervid gratitude of the queer little father, or to the white
liquor he had given him from a long-necked flask.

"It was awful hot stuff," he argued, "and he certainly did take on about it. Might have been her mother from the way he took on." Then he said "Foreigners," briefly, as though that explained it all, and went up to the tenement to change his wet clothes.

There was really no necessity for his sailing out to the *Liverpool* again. He knew that quite well as he beat uncertainly about in the wind. He knew the girl had recovered, for she had opened her eyes before he had left the boat, and had smiled up at her father; so there was absolutely no reason for his returning. Still, he argued, her father had asked him to do so — had, indeed, entreated him to let them see him again. Perhaps it was only his excitable Southern manner and meant nothing.

And then, again, he would not like them to go away thinking he had been ungracious and rude. They had asked him to come back to dinner, and it was even possible that they might at that moment be waiting for him. His hand pushed the tiller away, and then drew it back with a jerk, and threw the boat into the wind again. He would not go back. What right had he to go calling on strange girls, and "foreigners" at that? But as soon as he had determined he had no right to show this interest in an unknown woman, and that he would sail on to the pier, he put the boat sharply about, and headed it directly for the steamer. It seemed as if the boat did not go

fast enough, and in order that he might not again
change his intention he thought of the race he
had on with Robinson for the next Tuesday, and
had just determined that the stakes were not large
enough, and that he would demand more money,
when the sail of his cat-boat fluttered in the wind,
and left him at the foot of the *Liverpool's* ladder.

They were very glad to see him, and he felt
satisfied that he had come, and so expressed himself, and his pleasure in finding that the young
girl was not at all the worse in health for her
journey under the water. She said nothing to
this, but smiled upon him from beneath the long
lashes with dark, sleepy eyes. Her father seemed
to be a very pleasant little man for a " foreigner,"
with a great deal of manner, which compared
favorably with that of the Frenchman who taught
all the fashionable dances for fifty cents an hour,
and for nothing to those who formed classes of
six or over, at Sorley's Terrace Garden. Mr.
Burke could not remember having met with such
pleasant people before. They ate in the captain's
cabin in company with two of the ship's mates,
who were men of doubtful nationality, and who
said but little, but who regarded Mr. Burke closely, and drank frequently from the long-necked
bottle. The *Liverpool*, so they informed him,
was an English tramp steamer, chartered to carry
sewing-machines and other manufactured articles
to a port in Colombia, a South American repub-
lic, as they further explained. Señor Alvarez was

the owner of the cargo, and his daughter accompanied him for his better companionship and for a sight of the great city of New York. Mr. Burke, in turn, told them proudly of some of its wonders, and volunteered to show them its "sights." He thought they should certainly see Central Park' before they left, and "take in" a dance at the Terrace Garden. He would also be pleased to get them seats for the play then running at Niblo's, which was, so he understood, a "piece" worth seeing. His advances were received with polite consideration, but the señor regretted, in bad English but with perfect grace, their immediate departure. They had been lying for the past fortnight at the pier-head, and had but that morning anchored in the basin, to be in readiness to start with the tide at midnight. Mr. Burke received this information dumbly. He could not tell why, but he felt strangely hurt at their so soon going away. It was as if they had not only rejected him, but his rising feelings of friendliness and hospitality. But then, he answered himself, it could mean nothing to him whether they went or came. And yet when the dinner was over he was loath to go. He stood on the deck and pointed with his hand to the statue of Liberty on Bedlows Island.

"That's something youse ought'r see," he said, "but I guess you've been over it. No? It's a great bit of work inside, with stairs all the way up. You wouldn't think how big it is from here.

Why, mor'n a dozen men can stand on the ledge
round the hand. If you like," he added, consciously, "I'll sail you over there." He looked
at the señorita as he spoke, and she glanced at
her father, and he looked doubtfully at Burke,
at which the young man reddened, and then the
Spaniard, seeing this, told his daughter that she
should go of course, that it was most courteous
of the brave gentleman who had risked his life
for her. He himself could not attend them, as
there were clearing-papers to sign and a crew
to choose.

The sun was sinking over the Jersey flats when
they turned and headed back to the steamer.
The girl sat silently in the cross-seat amidships,
with one hand trailing in the water and with the
other shading her eyes. She wore a light dress,
open at the throat, and she had thrown a black
lace scarf over her head and shoulders, with one
end hanging. It served her for both head-dress
and shawl; and though Mr. Burke condemned it
as fantastic, he admitted that it was more be-
coming to her than Miss Casey's flat hat would
have been. They had passed the last two hours
together, stopping to rest on the grass around
the base of the statue, and watching the boats
of different make pass and repass the little isl-
and. It had seemed to Burke as if it were all
their own, as if the two of them had been cast
adrift there, and that the rest of the world had
gone on with its worries and business and mak-

ing of money and keeping of engagements without their caring or knowing. He looked with contempt upon the big ferry-boat that had to move on schedule time, and listened with a feeling of pity to the hoarse warnings of the tugs, and all the other whistles and bells that told of work and hurry. The strange girl at his side filled him with a feeling of distance from it all, her soft, lazy voice and slow speech, as she picked out and formed her sentences, quieted and soothed, and yet unsettled him. The places and things of which she spoke were so widely different from what he knew, and appeared, as she told of them, as though they must be so much richer and fuller and more plentiful. A land where it was always noon, with trees and flowers and clear skies, and where no one worked ; where the earth furnished food freely, and where the men seemed to do nothing all day but sit and smoke in the open squares ; where the nights were filled with music and dancing, and every one sat out-of-doors while the band played on the plaza.

"Yes," said Burke, breathing heavily, and staring down with a troubled look at the dark eyes of the girl stretched on the seat below him. "It sounds as if I'd like it. It ain't like this, is it?" he said, with a wave of his hand as a great flat scow, laden with freight cars, pushed past them with a panting tug at her side.

"Ah, yes ; but, however," said the girl, slowly, "you have that." She raised her arm from her side and stretched it out, with her long slim fingers pointing at the great bronze statue which stood out black against the red glow of the sunset.

"How?" said Burke; "have wot? I don't understand."

The girl rested her chin on her hand, and looked past him at the statue. Her lids closed heavily, so that he could hardly see her eyes. She shook her head. "You have liberty," she said, as though she were speaking to herself, "and freedom; you have it all. You have no tyrants in your country. It is all free and open and noble. With us there is no law. We are afraid to speak — we are afraid—" She stopped and closed her lips as though to compel herself to silence.

Burke watched her with a deep interest, which he believed was in what she said, but which was in the fact that she had said it. He waited for her to continue, but she remained silent.

"Wot do you mean?" he asked, softly. "Who's hurting you in Colombia?"

"We do not live in Colombia," she said. "Oh yes, the boat goes there, but our own home—the home I spoke of to you—is in Ecuador. There is peace in Colombia; but now with us there is war and revolution, and men are shot in the streets because they will not suffer to be robbed." She stopped again, and held her hands before her face.

"Shot in the street, eh?" said Mr. Burke, gravely. "Wot! Don't the police stop 'em?"

"It is a revolution," said the girl, impatiently.

" My people have been struggling for many years
against oppression. My uncle," she said, consciously, "should be President of Ecuador, but now because Gonzales has the army with him my uncle
cannot take his place, but hides in the mountains
without a home.· They hunt him like a bandit.
They have turned his house into a barracks for
Gonzales' soldiers. I myself saw their tents and
horses in the gardens where I have walked many
times. It is all confiscate—you understand?"

"Yes," said Burke, shaking his head solemnly.
"I read it in the papers. I read there was fighting going on down there; but I didn't take no
notice to it, it's so far away," he added, apologet-
ically.

"So far away!" the girl repeated, with quick
offence. "Do not men love their homes every-
where they may be? And love their free life,
and to—be masters? I and my people have had
no home for years; my uncle, chosen of the people, is driven from the city by a paid military; by
a man who robs the rich and taxes the poor—
taxes the salt they eat."

Mr. Burke reddened slowly. "Huh!" he said,
fiercely. "He does, hey? Well, wot are all your
men doing all this time?"

The girl gave him a quick look of approval.
She leaned forward, with her eyes fixed on his.
"They do the best they can," she said, slowly.
"They are poor, but not so poor but when they
get the guns and the cannons and the powder,

"BURKE WATCHED HER WITH A DEEP INTEREST"

like all that Gonzales has, they will not be poor
no more." She opened her clasped arms, and
threw her hands out with a quick, impulsive gesture. "Then the brother of my dear father," she
whispered, "will come back at the head of the
army to the people who have chosen him, and
those inside will open the gates, and he will march
in and drive Gonzales away, and Gonzales will
die, and there will be peace again and freedom,
and no more taxes, nor stealing, nor assassina-
tions." The tears came to her eyes and ran slowly down her cheeks, but she did not touch them.
"Ah, yes, we have brave men," she said, raising
her head proudly and nodding at him.

Burke shifted his hand on the tiller and looked
away. "And brave women, I guess," he said.
"I wish," he began—"I wish I could do something," he concluded, impotently.

The girl smiled quickly, and straightened her
head and shoulders. "Yes, I did not do wrong
to speak to you," she said, considering him with
grave, kind eyes. "You do understand it. You
are brave ; yes, you are brave, and you now know
what it is that we suffer."

Mr. Burke made no answer, but looked past and
beyond her. She seemed to have forgotten him
in the thoughts which her words had brought
back to her, and sat, with her chin on her hand,
gazing steadily across the water. It was all new
to him, and he let himself go for the time, and
did not try to shake off the hold the girl had

13

laid upon him. Mary Casey and her yellow hair
and proud nose, that was borne in air as the
daughter's of a janitor should be, grew familiar
and commonplace ; her complainings and up-
braidings returned to him with a jar, and he
compared, unwillingly enough, her love of the
gossip of the tenement and of the corner flirta-
tions, and her envy of other girls more fortunate
in richer young men, with this queer, beautiful
girl, who treated him as a hero, and whose life
seemed mixed up with danger and the making of
Presidents. He remembered with fresh regret
the lack of appreciation Miss Casey had shown
when he helped make a President by acting as
window - man at the last election. He was sure
this girl would have better understood the importance of that service.

Señor Alvarez received them at the head of the
accommodation-ladder, and bade Burke make the
boat fast. "You will remain to eat with us," he
said.

Burke did not argue with himself this time, but
told himself that this was for the last time, and
that he would never again see these strange people who had come so suddenly into his life.

The moon rose early that night, and by the
time they came out upon the deck had spread its
light over the river and softened the red and
green lights at the yards of the many steamers
anchored about them. It had turned the deck
white and the ratlines and cordage black, and

threw their shadows before them as they walked.
The Jersey shore lay like a black frame to the
picture, broken by blocks of blazing lights at the
ferries, which glowed like open fireplaces against
the dark background of the city. And to the
north the Battery showed a curve of lamps, and
high above it rose the Bridge like a great spider's
web, dotted with a double row of stars. But
Burke saw nothing of this; he was thinking of
the hot, restless country with the queer name,
many miles away, of which he had but just
learned, and yet for which he felt a fierce turmoil
of sympathy.

Though it was so late, the men were still lowering cases and boxes from the main-deck into
the open hatch with the aid of a creaking derrick,
and the three stood on the bridge and watched
them in silence. A mate, with his hands in the
pockets of his jacket, directed them in a low voice
and in a strange tongue, and the moonlight gave
to the men and their work a strange and unfamiliar aspect. The derrick swung short of the hatch,
and stopped with a jerk, and the box it had lifted
shook free from the rope about it, and came down,
turning over in the air. There was a warning cry
from the mate, and a crash as the box struck. It
burst into a dozen pieces, and there tumbled out
upon the moonlit deck a scattered mass of glittering sabres. Señor Alvarez uttered a quick, foreign oath, and threw himself in front of Burke,
as though to shut the sight from him; but Burke

only turned towards the girl and smiled in sympathy. The smile, more than anything else, seemed to startle the little Spaniard, and he glanced quickly at his daughter for a word of explanation.

"I have told him," she said. "I have told him much, and he guesses the rest."

"You have guessed? Yes," said Alvarez, fiercely; "what have you guessed?"

Burke shrugged his shoulders irresolutely. "It's no business of mine," he said. "I only wish it was," he added. He turned away, while the father and daughter spoke to each other quickly in their own language. Then the Spaniard turned and surveyed Burke with steady deliberation.

"You are a brave young man," he began, slowly, and speaking with soft intentness. "You have shown us to-day that you think of other lives before your own: is it not so? You have done very much for me: what will you do more?" He paused, dramatically, and held out his arms.

Burke regarded him with a troubled countenance. "What do you mean?" he asked.

"Come with us," urged the Spaniard, quickly. "That is what I mean. Come with us. My daughter, she has told me what you know. She did wrong to tell you, perhaps. We shall see. Perhaps no; perhaps she has done well. Come with us, and I will make you a captain. You will have many men under your command, and much of glory and reward, and when my brother is in the capital again, you will be a man with many titles

to honor, and a home for yourself with beautiful
gardens about it. We need brave men. You are
a brave man. Will you come?" The girl moved
slowly to her father, and stood beside him, with
one hand resting on his shoulder, and looked at
Burke from under the shadow of the black man-
tilla. He could see her eyes shining in the moonlight. They neither invited nor repelled him, but
questioned him earnestly. There was a moment's
pause, and then Burke shook himself and laughed
weakly. He thrust his hands deep into his pockets
and stood slouching, with his chin thrown out,
and smiling bitterly at the great buildings around
Bowling Green. "Well?" said the older man,
with sharp suspicion in his voice.

"You needn't think that— You can't understand," said Burke. "I am not good at saying
things," he added, impotently. "Wot I mean is,"
he began again, "you wouldn't understand, even
if I was to tell you."

"You have seen much," said the Spaniard,
slowly. "You know more than any man in this
country knows. My daughter, she has told you
why we come; you see for yourself why we come."
His voice rose to a sharp climax of excitement
and suspicious fear. "I make no more promises.
I command you. You understand, you *must* go
with us; you *must* go. We cannot trust you to
leave behind."

Burke's hands came out of his pockets with a
jerk. "Wot!" he growled, savagely. "You can't

trust me, can't you? Why not? Wot do you
know of wot I've got to do, of wot I'd like to do
if I had my way? I'm promised. I've given
my word to do something else. I'd like to fight
and row with the best of you—for you and for
the lady there. But — but I'm not free. I've
got my work cut out for me where I am. I've
got to stay here."

"You have got to stay here," repeated the
Spaniard, suspiciously. "Yet you are a young
man. You cannot have family or much business.
You take your pleasure swimming and sailing in
your boat in this bay. I have been informed so
of you since you were here this morning. All
these people know of you. They say you are very
brave, and that you are free. They all say good
of you, but now you know too much than is good
for you. You shall come with me."

Burke gave the girl a troubled glance and shook
his head. "Can't you understand?" he asked;
and then added, straightening himself and trying to give an air of importance to what he was
about to say, "I'm engaged."

"Engaged—what is that?" demanded the Spaniard, quickly.

"I'm engaged to be married to a young woman. I've got to stay at home and take care of
her."

The Spaniard regarded him closely for a moment with evident incredulity, and then burst
into a laugh which mocked him.

"Oh," he said, "it is that, is it? It is a young woman. It is *always* so. You have here honor, money, and much renown, and great good to do, and you remember this young woman. Let me not keep you!" he cried, with a sudden change of manner. "Let us not detain you from her any more. You are no doubt impatient to be back." He bowed with exaggerated courtesy, and, with an air of relief and amusement, moved backwards towards the top of the ladder. "Let us not keep you," he said, laughing.

Burke observed him with a sick feeling of rage at the injustice of it, and then raised his eyes slowly to those of the girl. She had turned from them, and was standing erect and motionless, with her hands resting on the polished rail and gazing steadily at the shore. She must surely understand, Burke thought.

"Perhaps," interrupted the mocking voice of the father—"perhaps it is that you do not desire to go for war. Fighting, it is true, is full of danger." He laughed and bowed again, motioning with a wave of the hand towards the ladder.

Burke turned and looked at him, with his shoulders bent and his head lowered. It reminded the Spaniard suddenly of a bull he had seen in the ring after the matadors had tormented it, and just before it had plunged forward and hurled a man lifeless against the President's box. He straightened himself, and fell back a step. "Perhaps," he said, quickly, "there is something I do not comprehend. You will pardon me, but I misunderstood."

Burke regarded him steadily for some short time, and then turned away without having heard what he had said. He slipped his cap from his head, and moved a step nearer the girl. "It isn't that I am afraid of the fighting—*you* know that," he said—"but that I am afraid of something else." He stopped and stood with his eyes fixed so earnestly on the girl's face that she seemed to feel them, and her shoulders moved slightly as though the cool night air had made her tremble. "I am afraid of breaking my promise that's given," he said. He waited a moment, but the girl did not move, or show by any sign that she had heard him. "I can't do that," he begged. His voice was full of doubt and trouble. "I can't do that, can I?" The girl still stood motionless, and then shrugged her shoulders slightly, and turned out the palms of her hands. Burke drew a long breath, and straightened himself resolutely.

"Good-by," said Burke.

She put her hand out slowly, and barely touched it to his own, and then walked the short length of the bridge away from him. He went down the ladder and over the side without looking back again, and dropped into his boat. He had gone up the ladder so proudly that morning, and now the world and all the world's ways seemed ajar and devious, and his reason neither applauded him for having made a sacrifice, nor assured him that he had done well.

As his boat rounded the bow of the steamer, a row-boat shot out from under her side, and its solitary occupant pulled off with short, quick strokes for the shore. It was the sudden sight of Burke's boat and the sail looming white in the moonlight that had startled him, and Burke, recognizing this, called to him to stop. The oarsman answered with a quicker pull on the oar, and bowed his head as if to hide his face from observation. Burke shortened sail, and in a moment drew up at the row-boat's side. "Oh, it's you, is it?" he said. "You" was Mr. "Big" Marks.

Mr. Marks was the proprietor of a sailors' lodging-house, who robbed his lodgers, and as a return helped them to rob their vessels; who smuggled in a small way, and even, it is said, was not too proud to stoop to inform on other gentlemen who smuggled in a larger away.

"Give me your rope," commanded Mr. Burke. "I'll tow ye in."

The man in the boat sat motionless. "You needn't mind me, Hefty," he whined, humbly. "I'm just rowing about; I can get in by myself."

Mr. Burke regarded him with steady scrutiny. "You're lying," he said; "give me that rope. Wot was ye doing under the bow of that steamer? and," he continued, angrily, "wot did you try to get away from me so fast for?"

Mr. Marks threw him his painter, and crawled over the side of the cat-boat. "One of my men," he began, glibly enough, "is on the *Liverpool;* he's a Swede that's a regular customer of mine when he's in port. I just rowed out to see him off. They get away in an hour or two."

"In an hour," corrected Burke. He looked back at the steamer with heavy eyes, and seemed for the moment to have forgotten his sudden animosity towards his prisoner. Seeing which, Mr. Marks lit a cigar, and offered another with a propitiatory smile to Burke.

"It's good," he said; "it's never seen no custom-house."

"I'm not smoking," said Burke, grimly.

"Training again, hey?" asked Mr. Marks, pleasantly. "Well, my money is on you this time, and every time. There ain't none of 'em as can touch you—that's what *I* say."

Burke made no reply to this, but gazed at his companion with stern inquiry and with troubled eyes. He did not speak again until they had reached the wharf, and then, as Mr. Marks started away with a hasty "good-night," he called sharply after him : "Come back here. I want you."

Mr. Marks hesitated, and then turned, and waited with evident uneasiness.

"You'll come and take a drink," said Burke.

Mr. Marks fingered the cigar in his hand nervously. "I'd like to, Hefty," he said, "but another time. I've got to see a man at the place. I've

got an appointment with him. Some other night
—hey? Got to hurry now."

"I'll go with you," said Burke, steadily.

Mr. Marks looked at him for the first time with
sharp scrutiny, and laughed a low, comfortless
laugh. He was a fat, oily person, with a face
reddened by drink and the wind of the river.
Burke towered beside him as they walked along,
his face set and miserable. From one place to
another and from one street corner to the next
the two men walked and halted. Sometimes to
speak to an acquaintance, sometimes to order
something to drink, which both left untasted on
the bar. As the hour wore on the nervousness
of the older man became obvious, and at last, in
a saloon near the Battery, he slipped quickly
through a side entrance and ran into the night.
The next moment Burke was at his side.

"Here, you had better not try that on," he
growled, and dropped into step again.

Mr. Marks stopped and drew a long breath.
"Well, you make me tired, Burke," he said, des-
perately. It was his first sign of rebellion, and
Burke welcomed it. "What are you after, hey?"
Marks demanded. "What is it going to be?
You're stopping all my fun," he went on, fiercely,
"and you don't seem to be getting anything out
of it yourself. What do you want of me, anyway, trailing me all over the place?"

They were at the end of a pier and quite alone.
Burke looked about him carefully, and then turned

towards the water where the *Liverpool* lay, a black, dim silhouette in the moonlight. The night mist was rising and it was growing colder. The place was quite deserted.

"Oh," said Burke, with unaffected carelessness, "I don't know wot you are up to, and I'll stay by you till I do. That's all."

Mr. Marks regarded him with fierce suspicion, and broke the silence at last with an angry oath. "I suppose you want me to divide — hey ?" he cried, viciously. He looked at his watch, and snapped the lid with a sharp click. "It's that or letting it all go," he said. "Curse you for a meddling fool!" He stamped his feet and clinched his fat hands impotently. "I'd ha' been aboard her by this time if it hadn't been for you."

Burke raised his eyes slowly towards the steamer, and saw that the smoke was coming out of the *Liverpool's* funnel in a thick black cloud. It gave his heart a sudden sharp wrench, and he glanced about him with a look which sobered his companion instantly.

"See here, Hefty, my lad," he whined, in a low, conciliatory tone, "we've got to work quick if we're going to stop her. They've got the anchors up now, most like. Here," he exclaimed, with an apparent burst of generosity, "I'll tell you what I'll do. I'll go halves with you—that's three thousand dollars sure. Three thousand— think of that. It's a fortune."

Burke regarded him with a look of slow amazement. "Three thousand dollars," he said, stupidly.

"Yes, easy that," begged the other. "There's twelve thousand dollars' worth of stuff on her altogether, counting the Hotchkiss guns and the ammunition. The informer gets half. That's *law*. There's no getting out of that. It's *law*. They've *got* to give it to you, and it's honest money, too. What right have them half-breeds coming up here involving us Americans in their d——d revolutions ? It's against the courtesy of nations— that's what it is. I read it all up, and I know what I'm givin' ye. They can't do it. Look at the *Alliance* case, and the *Mary Miller*. Levy got five thousand dollars for giving *her* away, and I'd ha' pulled six thousand out of this if you'd let me alone. Well, speak up ; what do you say ?"

Burke was leaning forward, with his eyes staring into those of his companion. He was breathing heavily. "Wot are you going to do ?" he asked, quietly. His voice was low and uncertain.

Marks caught him familiarly by the sleeve. " Do ?" he asked, trembling with excitement ;— " go to the *Washington*—she's at her slip there beyond the fire-boat—and tell the captain what we know. He can stop her before she reaches the lower bay, and he may if he believes what we say. And he has got to believe me, because one of the crew give me all the figures, and where they got the stuff, and who paid for it. It's Alvarez himself, the brother to the one they run out of the country — him as wants to be President. Come !" he cried, frantically, and dancing from one foot to the other in his excitement.

But Burke stood still, regarding him stupidly. "Three thousand dollars. For me," he said. "I don't understand."

"Hully gee !" cried the other. "Don't I tell you we get half ! The government gets one-half the cargo and the informer gets the rest. That's the law. Think of it — three thousand dollars ! Why, man alive, you can marry on that ; and it's good money too, come by honest for serving your country. Old man Casey will be proud of you, Hefty—and—and Mary too, hey, she—"

"Shut up !" said Burke, savagely. He glanced with a troubled look to where the revenue-cutter *Washington* lay at the end of the Barge Office dock. It was so very near. He stood rigid, breathing quickly, and with only his fingers working at his side. The other watched him with evil, wide-open eyes. Then Burke gave a short gasp of relief, and, reaching out suddenly, caught Marks by the sleeve. "Come with me," he said, steadily. "Come over here and sit down."

"Sit down ? Like hell !" cried the the other fearfully. "What ails you ? Don't you see she's got steam on now ? She'll be out of the river before—"

"You're not going to the *Washington*," said

Burke. "You're not going to give nothing away.
You are going to stay here with me. There's
—there's friends of mine on board that boat.
They're not hurting you, and you're not going to
hurt them, nor interfere with them neither—see?
You'll stay right here." Mr. Marks's face was
black, and the muscles working with excitement
and the fear of losing what he already considered
his. "I mean," said Burke, firmly, "that you're
going to stay here until that boat gets out of the
harbor, till she gets clean off. Do you understand? That's wot I mean."

"Oh," said the other, softly, "that's what you
mean, is it?"

He jerked his sleeve away, and his arm rose
suddenly in the air, and Burke caught it by the
wrist and tripped him up with a quick jerk that
threw him heavily over on his back. Burke threw
himself on his chest and wrenched at the knife in
his hand.

"You would, would you," he said, under his
breath. "Give it up—do you hear? Give it up,"
he growled, "or I'll—"

The fat little man beneath him groaned and
struggled helplessly under his weight. "Let me
up," he gasped, "I'm choking—let me up."

Burke tossed the knife into the river, and settled his fingers carefully round the other's throat.
"Lie still," he whispered. "If you yell or nothing I'll choke the life out of you and leave you
lying here—"

But even as he uttered this threat Mr. Burke raised his eyes to the bay, and gave a soft low cry. The smoke was pouring in a black mass from the funnel of the *Liverpool*, and as he watched her she started slowly forward, as a sled slides over the ice, and then moved more and more swiftly until the smoke stood out in a straight line and she grew less and less distinct, until, after passing the base of the great statue of Liberty, she disappeared into the mist and out of his sight forever.

The man beneath him groaned feebly and cursed him under his breath.

"You can get up," said Burke, gently, with his eyes still staring into the mist. "She's gone now."

"Silly sort of a play, I call it," said Van Bibber, as they left the theatre.

"I don't know," his friend dissented, slowly. "Why?"

"Well, about that letter, for instance," Van Bibber continued. "The idea of a girl throwing a man over like that just because some one sent her an anonymous letter about him! Of course, if she'd really cared for the man she'd have given him a chance to explain; she wouldn't have believed it at once. Still," he added, magnanimously, "if she *had* asked him about it there wouldn't have been any more play. The author had to do something."

But Travers disagreed. "Oh, I don't know," he said. "I think it's very true to life myself. I know I'd hate to have any one writing letters like that about me."

Van Bibber laughed easily. "Nice sort of friends you have," he said.

"They're your friends."

"Some of them are," Van Bibber corrected; "but I think better of them than you do, apparently. I'm sure I'm willing you should write all

14

the anonymous letters to them you please about me."

"That," said Travers, mockingly, "is because you're so good."

"Not at all," Van Bibber answered, hotly. "It isn't whether the letter told the truth; the point is that the girl is willing to believe it. That's what I object to. That's where the chap who wrote the play shows that he doesn't know anything about women."

"Well, as I said," Travers repeated, stubbornly, "I think you are altogether wrong. She acted just as any of the girls we know would have acted, and, as I said, I should hate to have any one write a letter like that to my friends."

"And as I said," reiterated Van Bibber, warmly, "you can write all the letters you choose about me, and my friends can stand it, and so can I."

Travers stopped and looked back over his shoulder as they mounted the steps of the club. "Do you mean that?" he asked, seriously.

"I do," said Van Bibber, laughing. Then they went into the club, and scowled at all the other men as though they were intruders, and talked about deviled kidneys.

Van Bibber slept peacefully that night in spite of the deviled kidneys, but Travers sat up until late composing an anonymous letter, which he hoped would fall like a bomb-shell into the camp of his friends. The morning found him still intent upon it and mischief, and by the time he had finished breakfast his plans of campaign were already made.

He first went to a type-writer in one of the big hotels, and dictated four letters to him announcing the date of a women's meeting for a charitable purpose. The envelopes for these were addressed to four different women. He tore up the letters when he reached the street, but put the envelopes with their non-committal type-written addresses in his pocket. On Sixth Avenue he purchased a half-dozen sheets of cheap paper, and carried them to his room, where he locked himself in, and wrote with his left hand, on four separate sheets, the following communication:

"DEAR MADAM,—When Mr. Van Bibber calls on you again, ask him how well he knows Maysie Lindsey. If he denies knowing her, ask him to show you the tintype of the woman which he wears in a locket on a chain about his neck.

"A FRIEND."

"There," said Travers, proudly, "I think that is calculated to spread doubt and confusion in the stoutest heart." He put the letters in the envelopes with the type-written addresses, and posted them that same morning. Then he wrote to Van Bibber, and told him of what he had done.

"And I call it a piece of damned impertinence," said that gentleman that same evening.

"You're afraid now," said Travers, easily.

"Last night you could trust your friends better than I could; now you're afraid."

"That's not it," said Van Bibber. "I *can* trust them. I don't care what you said about *me*, but by sending letters like that to those girls you intimated that they take an interest in me, that they are more or less concerned about me, which is a piece of presumption I wouldn't be guilty of myself, and a thing which you had no business to assume. Suppose they find out that you wrote those letters, they'll ask me: 'Why did he send one to me? What have I to do with you? Why should I care what women you know or don't know?' It was impertinent to them, that's what I say. You can leave me out of it entirely, but you had no business to put them in the light of caring about me."

"But they do care about you, don't they?" Travers asked, innocently.

"That's not for me to say, nor you. I'm ashamed of you. Practical joking is all very well between idiots like ourselves, but you had no business to drag women into it."

"Well," sighed Travers, "you can't make me rude by being rude yourself, you know. You told me distinctly that I could write the letter, and I have written it, and if you've any confidence in your friends you will do nothing about it, but let them work it out their own way. I call it a most excellent test of their confidence. You ought to be obliged to me for giving you such a chance of finding out what dear good friends you have."

"I shall treat the whole thing with absolute contempt, as they will," said Van Bibber, stiffly. "It is beneath my notice, and so are you. Maysie Lindsey, indeed! Who the devil is Maysie Lindsey?"

"I don't know," said Travers, pleasantly. "She is merely a beautiful creature of my imagination. Rather pretty name, I think, don't you?—Maysie Lindsey." Then he asked, with a touch of misgiving, "You don't *happen* to wear anything around your neck, do you?"

"Certainly not, confound you!" said Van Bibber.

Van Bibber had as large a nodding acquaintance with men in New York as almost any other man in it, but the women he knew were not so many and much more near. The four women of whom he saw the most were those to whom Travers had sent the anonymous letters. He was in the habit of seeing them at their own houses and at other people's houses as often as once a week or more frequently, and he decided that instead of writing them at once, and explaining that a friend of his had sent them an anonymous letter about him, and that he begged that they would overlook the impertinence, he would wait until he saw them and then explain the situation verbally. But as the week wore on, the temptation to let the matter take its course got the better of his first determination, and his curiosity and his desire to see just how far his friends trusted him overcame his original purpose of setting things right.

Mrs. "Jimmy" Floyd was from one of the Western cities; she had married Floyd while abroad and had entered into the life of New York with all the zeal and enthusiasm of a new convert. She had adapted herself to her surroundings, though she had not herself been adopted. But now she was undoubtedly an important personage, and very many people paid court to her, not for herself so much as for what she could do for them. There were a number of men to whom she was at home every day after five, and Van Bibber came to see her then very frequently. She knew him well enough to ask him to fill a place when some one had failed her, and he thought her amusing, but only that. He had a youthful horror of having it thought that he was attached to married women, and made it a rule to come late in the afternoon and to be among the first to go. Owing to this no one had ever found him or left him with Mrs. Floyd, and the men, especially those whom he allowed to outstay him, were grateful to him in consequence. Her drawing-room was a place for gossip, and Van Bibber told her once that he came because it saved him from reading the papers, and that if she would fine herself a penny every time she or her friends said "I suppose you have heard," she would be able to pay for a box at the Horse Show with the money. He

called there a week after Travers had sent forth
his letters, and found her for the first time alone.
When she nodded to him brightly, and told the
servant in the same breath that she was not at
home to any one else, Van Bibber smiled grimly
to himself and regarded her with a masklike
countenance. He saw that he had been trapped
into a tête-à-tête, and that one of the letters had
evidently reached the home of the Floyds.

Mrs. Floyd's attitude as she sank back in her
cushions was an unsettled one, and her whole manner expressed pleasurable expectancy. Her visit-
or observed this with amused disapprobation, but
as she seemed so happy in believing what she had
read of him, he thought it would be rather a pity
to spoil her enjoyment of it by telling her the
truth.

"Well," she said, "and what have you been doing with yourself lately?" She spoke quite gayly, as though her recently acquired knowledge of
him gave to whatever he might have to say a fresh
interest.

Van Bibber observed this also with a cynical
sense of amusement, and saw that she had placed
him under the light of a standing lamp, which
threw his face into strong relief, while hers was
in shadow. "Just," as he said later to Travers,
"as though she were keeping a private detective
agency." The talk between Mrs. Floyd and her
visitor ran on unevenly. She was eager to question him, and yet afraid of being too precipitate,

and he was standing on his guard.   At last something he said of a young Frenchman visiting the
city seemed to give her the chance she wanted.

"Oh yes," she commented, indifferently, "I remember him at Homburg.   He is rather a sentimental youth, I fancy.   He wears a bangle, and
a chain around his neck.   We could see them
when he played tennis."

Van Bibber gazed thoughtfully into the open
fire.   "Yes," he said, politely.

Mrs. Floyd looked at the fire also.   She was
afraid she had begun too clumsily, and yet she
still continued recklessly in the same opening.
"It is rather feminine in a man, I think ; not un-
manly exactly, either, but rather a pose, like writing in a diary.   You pretend that you write it
without thinking of any one's seeing what you
have written, but you always have the possibility
in your mind, don't you ?   And men always know
that some day some one will see their bangle
or their locket.   They think it gives them a
mysterious or sentimental interest.   Don't you
think so ?"

Van Bibber changed his gaze from the fire to
the point of his shoe, and then, as an idea came
to him suddenly, smiled wickedly.   He looked up
as quickly to see if Mrs. Floyd had noticed his
change of expression, and then relapsed into gloom
again.   "The only man I know who goes in for
that sort of thing," he said, "is Travers.   Travers
wears a gold chain around *his* neck, and he keeps it

on all the time. I've seen it at the Racquet Club.
There is a picture of a girl on one side, a tintype,
and on the other, two initials in diamonds. The
initials are M. L."

"M. L. !" exclaimed Mrs. Floyd, confusedly.

"In diamonds," added Van Bibber, impressively.

"M. L. in diamonds ! Why," Mrs. Floyd exclaimed, "that's —" and then correcting herself
midway, she added, tamely, "that's very curious."

"Curious ?" asked Van Bibber, politely. "Why
curious ? They're not your initials, are they ?"

"I was told," said Mrs. Floyd, seriously, "that
is—some one told me," she began again, "that *you*
wore a locket just like that around *your* neck."

"Fancy !" said Van Bibber, with a gasp of
amusement. "Who told you that, if I may ask ?"

"No one that you know," Mrs. Floyd replied,
hastily. "But he must have confused you two ;
don't you suppose that is it ? It is because you
are so much together."

"Told you I wore a locket around my neck ?"
repeated Van Bibber, with some severity. "How
absurd ! It is very evident that he has mixed us
up. We don't look much alike, do we ? Perhaps
he saw us at a Turkish bath. Every man looks
like every other one when he is wrapped in a cloud
of steam and a bath robe. Only the other day I
took old man Willis for an attendant, and told
him to hurry up my coffee. I suppose that's how
it happened. You had better ask Travers about

it next time he comes and see what he says.   He'll deny it, probably ; but I assure you I have seen it ; so you can charge him with it with perfect safety."

Mrs. Floyd looked at Van Bibber doubtfully for a moment, but he returned her look with a smile of such evident innocence that she smiled in return, and then they both laughed together.

"And I thought it was you all the time," she said.   "What an odd mistake !"

"Very humorous indeed," said Van Bibber. He rose, and Mrs. Floyd made no effort to detain him.   Her suddenly acquired interest in him had departed.   "Don't forget the initials," said Van Bibber.

"I shall not," Mrs. Floyd answered, laughing. "I shall remember."

"And in diamonds, too," added Van Bibber, as he bowed at the door.

Miss Townsend was a young woman who took everything in life seriously but herself.   She was irritatingly but sincerely humble when her own personality was concerned, and was given to considering herself an unworthy individual only fit to admire the actions of real personages.   She received deserved compliments either mockingly or as sarcasms at her expense, and made her friends indignant by waxing enthusiastic over people whom they did not consider one-fourth as worthy of such enthusiasm as she was herself.   She was a

very loyal friend, and when she was with Van Bibber had the tact not to talk of those things which
might be beyond his reach. Still, when she did
venture with him on those matters of life and
conscience and conduct which most interested her,
she found his common-sense and his sense of humor vastly disturbing to her theories. She received him this afternoon with a preoccupied air,
which continued until her mother, who had been
with her when he had entered, had left the room.

"I do not know how soon I shall have the
chance to see you alone again," she began at once,
"and I have something to say to you. I have
thought it over for some time, and I have considered it very seriously ; I think I am doing the
right thing, but I cannot tell."

Van Bibber wanted to assure her that it was
not to be taken seriously, and felt fresh indignation that she should have been troubled so impu-
dently. But he only said "yes," sympathetically,
and waited.

"I want to ask you," she said, regarding him
with earnest eyes, "if you know that you have an
enemy."

Van Bibber bit his lips to hide a smile, and felt
even more ashamed of himself for smiling. "Oh
dear, no," he said, "of course not. We don't have
enemies nowadays, do we ? There are lots of people who don't like one, I suppose ; but enemies
went out of date long ago, with poisoned cups and
things like that, didn't they ?"

"No; you are wrong," she said. "There is some one who dislikes you very much, who wants to injure you with your friends, and who goes about doing it in a mean and cowardly way. In so low a way that I should not notice it at all; and then again I think that it is my duty to tell you of it, so that you can be on your guard, and that you may act about it in whatever way you think right. That is what I have been trying to decide: whether I am a better friend if I say nothing, or whether I ought to speak and warn you." She stopped, quite breathless with anxiety, and Van Bibber felt himself growing red. "What do you think?" she said.

"Oh, I don't know," said Van Bibber, unhappily. "Suppose you tell me all about it. Of course, whatever you do would be the right thing," he added. She put her hand in the pocket of her frock, and drew out a letter with a type-written address. Van Bibber anathematized Travers anew at the sight of it.

"Last week," Miss Townsend began, impressively, "I received this letter. It is an anonymous letter about you. What it says does not concern me or interest me in the least. That is what I want you to understand. No matter what was said of one of my friends, if it came to me in such a way, it could not make the least difference to me. Of course I would not for an instant consider anything from such a source, but the point, in my mind, is that some one is trying to do you

"'DO YOU KNOW THAT YOU HAVE AN ENEMY?'"

harm, and that it is my duty to let you know of
it. Do you understand?" Van Bibber guiltily
bowed his head in assent. "Then here it is," she
said, handing him the offensive letter as though it
were a wet and dirty rag. "Don't open it here,
and never speak to me of it again. If you did—
if you explained it or anything, I would feel that
you did not believe me when I say that I believe
in you, and that I only speak of this thing at all
because I want to put you on your guard. Some
man, or some woman more likely, has written this
to hurt you with me. He or she has failed. That
is the point I want you to remember, and I hope
I have done right in speaking of it to you. And
now," she exclaimed with a sigh of relief, and
with a sudden wave of her hands, as if she were
throwing something away, "*that* is over."

Van Bibber's first impulse was to put the letter
in the fire, and tell her the truth about it; but his
second thought was that this girl had for a week
been considering as to how she could act in his
best interest, and that to show her now that she
had been made a joke of would be but a poor return of her thoughtfulness of him. So he placed
the letter in his pocket, and thanked her for her
warning, and sincerely for her confidence, and
went away. And as he left the house his sense
of pleasure in the thought that his friend trusted
him was mixed with an unholy desire to lay hands
upon Travers. He determined to end and clear
up the matter that afternoon, at once and for-

ever, and with that object in view took a hansom to the house of Miss Edith Sargent.

Miss Sargent was a friend of both Travers and himself. She was an unusual girl, and the fact that she was equally liked by men and women proved it. She frequently regretted she had not been born a boy, and tried to correct this injustice by doing certain things better than most men could do them, and so gained their admiration. Van Bibber agreed with her that it was a pity that she was not a man, as, so he explained it, there were too few attractive men, while there were so many attractive women that it kept him continually in trouble. Miss Sargent was the president of a society for the lower education of women, the members of which were required to know as much about polo as they did of symbolic and impressionist pictures, and were able to keep quite separate the popular violinist or emotional actress of the day as a person from the same individual as an artist; they did not sob over the violinist's rendering of music which some one else had written, on one afternoon, and then ask him to tea the next. They did not live on their nerves or on their feelings, but on their very rich fathers, on whom they drew heavily for gowns, hunters, and pianos, on which last they could play passably well themselves.

Travers, it was believed, was sentimentally content that Edith Sargent had been born a girl, and spoke of her as Miss Sargent, and not as Edith

Sargent, as the other men did. Van Bibber considered this a very dangerous sign.

Miss Edith Sargent was getting out of her
brougham as Van Bibber drew up in his hansom. She greeted him brightly with a nod, and
told him that she was half frozen, and that he
was just in time for some tea. He waited until
she gave some directions to the footman for the
evening and then walked up the steps beside her.

"You've saved me from writing you a note,"
she said. "I wanted to see you about getting up
a coaching-party for the game on Thanksgiving
Day. Do you think it's too late?"

Van Bibber observed her covertly, but she did
not seem to be conscious of anything beyond
what she was saying, and regarded him frankly
and without embarrassment. He decided that
she had not received the letter, and felt a tempo-
rary sense of relief.

"It is rather late," he said; "most of the
coaches are engaged so far ahead, you know; but
we might be able to get a private one."

They walked into the drawing-room together,
and she threw her sable boa and muff on the divan and went to the fire to warm her fingers.

"Whom could we ask?" she said. Van Bibber was regarding her so intently that she stopped
and looked up at him curiously. "Whom could
we ask?" she repeated, and added, after a pause,
"You're not listening to what I'm saying."

They continued looking at each other for a short moment, and then the girl, with a sudden exclamation of intelligence, walked back into the library beyond, returning with an envelope in her hand. Van Bibber saw that the address upon it was type-written.

"Here's that letter you and Travers sent me," she said. She put it in his hand and left him standing gazing dumbly down at it, while she returned to the open fire and stretched her fingers out before it. As he continued silent, she turned and looked over her shoulder at him, and then, as she caught his look of embarrassment, laughed easily at the sight of it. "Don't you think," she said, "it's about time you two became accustomed to the fact that you have grown up?"

Van Bibber gazed at her blankly and shook his head. "Travers told you," he said, ruefully.

"Travers told me!" she repeated with disdain. "You both told me. I do hope I've intelligence enough to keep up with you two and your games and foolishnesses. There's no one else who would do anything so silly." She laughed a triumphant, mocking laugh. "You and your Maysie Lindsey and gold lockets, you're a pretty trio, aren't you? And you thought you were going to have such a fine joke on me. Oh, you're so clever, you two; you're so deep and subtle. How long have you ceased wearing velvet suits and red sashes?"

"That's all right," said Van Bibber, sulkily,

"but I want you to know I've had trouble enough about this thing, and it's all Travers'—"

"There is some other game, perhaps," she said, nodding her head at him, "that you play better than this."

"Oh, I'm going," said Van Bibber. He stopped at the door and shook his high hat at her impressively. "If you have any regard for your young friend Travers," he said, "you'd better send him word to keep out of my way for a week or two."

"Wait and have some tea," she called after him, but Van Bibber pulled open the front door, and as he did so heard an echo of mocking laughter and something that sounded like "Give my love to Maysie Lindsey."

There was still one other girl to see, and Van Bibber kicked viciously at the snow at the thought of it as he strode hurriedly towards her house. He wished that he might find her out; but she was in, the man said, and she herself said that she was glad to see him.

Miss Norries was a peculiarly beautiful girl, who almost succeeded in living in a way that was worthy of her face. If she did not do so, it was not through lack of effort on her own part. And yet to others there seemed to be no effort; people said of her that she had been born fine and good, and could not be otherwise had she tried. "It is only we poor souls who know what temptation is," they said, "that deserve credit for overcoming it. Grace Norries always does the right

15

thing because she doesn't know there is any other thing to do."

But Miss Norries had her own difficulties. She had once said to Van Bibber, "The trouble is that there are so many standards, even among one's best friends, among the people that you respect most, that it makes it hard to keep to one's own."

To which Van Bibber had replied, flippantly: "*You* have no right to complain. All you have to do when you get up in the morning is to look in the glass and say, 'To-day I must live up to *that.*' It's a pretty high standard to live up to, I know, but it's all your own." At which Miss Norries had gazed coldly at nothing, and Van Bibber had wished he had not complimented her on the one thing for which she could not possibly take any credit.

She received him now graciously, as a much older woman might have done, but told him he could not stay, as she had to dress for dinner.

"It won't take long to say what I came to say," Van Bibber answered her. "I came on purpose to say it, though. It's rather serious— at least, it didn't start out so, but it's getting serious." He did not look at her, but at the fire, as though he were trying to draw confidence from it. But his anxiety was unnecessary, for Miss Norries regarded him tranquilly and without loss of her usual poise. She was always ready to laugh with those who laughed, or to weep with those who wept, giving out just enough of her own personality to make her sympathy of value, and yet never allowing it to carry her away.

"Perhaps," said Van Bibber, with a sudden inspiration, "you have something to say to me."

"No, I don't know that I have," the girl answered, considering. "Has anything happened? I mean, is there anything I ought to speak about that I haven't? Are you to be congratulated or condoled with? Is that it?"

"Well, you ought to know," Van Bibber answered, "whether I am to be condoled with or not. I'm certainly not to be congratulated."

"I don't understand," she said, smiling.

"Oh, well, then," he exclaimed, with a sigh of relief, "it's probably all right. Only I thought you would have received it by this time, and if you had, I wanted to explain. But if you haven't received it you probably won't now, and so I needn't say anything about it."

"Received what?" asked Miss Norries, with a perplexed laugh. "But," she added, "if you don't wish to speak of it we will talk of something I do understand. Oh, you mean the package of books you sent me. I ought to have written you about them. They were just the ones I wanted. I was so very—"

"Books! no," said Van Bibber, with disgust. "It's a letter," he blurted out. "Some one told me—at least I happened to find out—that some one sent you an anonymous letter about me. And I thought you might have received it, and—"

He stopped in some confusion, for he liked Miss Norries better than he did the other women, and he found it, for some reason, harder to talk to her about the letter than to those others.

"Yes, I received it," she said.

He looked at her a moment with startled surprise.

"No!" he exclaimed. "You don't say so! You did receive it? Well, but then — I don't understand. Why didn't you tell me?"

"Tell you what?" said Miss Norries, gently, but with some hauteur. "Why should I speak to you of it? I do not see that it concerns you. It was an anonymous letter addressed to me, and I threw it in the fire." She looked at him inquiringly for a moment, and then turned her attention to the falling snow against the window.

"Yes, I know," said Van Bibber, thinking very fast and talking to make time, "but the letter was about me, you know, and suggested—that is, it put me in rather an unpleasant light."

The girl gave a slight laugh of annoyance and stood up. "I fail to see how it concerns you," she said. "It was insulting to me, that's all. I did not consider it further than that. What it said about you has nothing whatever to do with it that I can see. All that I could understand was that some one had tried to annoy me by sending me an anonymous letter." She stopped and smiled. "You must have a rather poor opinion of yourself and your friends if you think they consider you and anonymous letters with equal seriousness. Now you have to go," she added, "or I shall be late. Thank you ever so much for the books, and come in to-morrow early, and tell me what you think about them ; but now I really must hurry, so good-bye."

Van Bibber put his hat firmly on his head as he went down the steps, and then turned and gazed at the closed door of the house he had just left with a look of settled bewilderment. "Well," he said, with a sigh, "it's all part of the dáy's work, I suppose. For which," he added, impressively, "Travers will have to pay."

A long dinner and a large open fire in the almost deserted club had melted his anger by ten o'clock to such a degree that Travers ventured to ask for the details of the day's adventure, and Van Bibber was so far pacified as to give them.

"Well, I must say," declared Travers, rubbing his knees and gazing with much satisfaction into the open fire, "it turned out to be a very interesting experiment, didn't it ? But it hasn't proved anything that I can see. I don't see that it has shown which of the girls cares the most about you, has it ? What do you think ?"

"I don't know," said Van Bibber, lowering his voice and glancing over his shoulder. "Which do you think, now ?"